THE EARL'S CHRISTMAS CONSULTANT

FLORA HAS MASQUERADED as a French maid for years. Though she despises hiding her skill at the piano and has no innate fondness for mending, she is happy to no longer be on the run. When a handsome earl who sent butterflies fluttering through her chest as a child discovers her French is atrocious, Flora requires a new position, lest her true identity be discovered.

Christmas has never been Lord Wolfe McIntyre's favorite season. His parents never celebrated it, and he never imagined he would succumb to sentimentality as an adult. After all, he runs a gaming hell. But when his sister's engagement is broken, Wolfe vows to host a magnificent holiday ball so she can find a husband before the next season. The only problem? His lack of knowledge about the holiday.

Wolfe is shocked when his friend's maid appears at his manor house in Scotland. When he hired a Christmas consultant, he expected a stern Bavarian woman with a knowledge of Yule logs, not an alluring young woman whom he last saw claiming a blatantly false identity and who seems distressed at seeing him. Wolfe is even more shocked when he discovers he... desires her. Earls are not supposed to find their servants appealing, no matter how much they fill their homes with Yuletide joy and music. But perhaps there's a reason Flora looks familiar...

Other books in the *Wedding Trouble* series:
Don't Tie the Knot
Dukes Prefer Bluestockings
The Earl's Christmas Consultant
How to Train a Viscount
A Kiss for the Marquess
A Holiday Proposal

CHAPTER ONE

THE DRAWING ROOM WAS empty, the townhouse quiet, but Flora tiptoed over dark wooden floorboards and sumptuous Persian rugs. She did not linger at the Duke of Vernon's collection of glistening china or at the immaculate portraits of people who would be horrified to discover her in the duke's parlor. The ebony and ivory keys of the piano gleamed enticingly from one corner of the room, but Flora settled instead in an armchair, conscious the velvet upholstery and gilded fluting were intended for aristocrats and not servants.

Flora removed a book she'd hidden with her sewing. Her heart thrummed a nervous rhythm, and she fought her inclination to flee. Flora favored working in the quiet of her bedroom, but that would leave her subject to discovery. Servant quarters offered little privacy. The other servants would gossip if they read the title of her book, and that was an impossibility.

The book's scarlet binding glared at her. *La Grammaire Française.* Flora opened it and forced herself to study the rows of nouns and verbs.

If only she'd devoted time to French when she was younger.

If only she hadn't convinced her father to let her pursue Italian.

If only she hadn't needed to acquire a new identity, and if only she hadn't chosen to pretend to be a French maid.

The only thing anyone knew about her was that she was French. How could she admit her lie?

Feigning being French had seemed clever. What better way to explain a lack of references than to declare herself a refugee? And what better way to ensure her identity remain secret than to give herself a new name and a new past?

Now Flora was no longer a maid in a vicarage in Norfolk, but a lady's maid to a duchess in the very capital in which her father had died. Even worse, the Duchess of Vernon intended to move to Guernsey with her husband, and she'd hinted frequently at the large number of French speakers on the island.

No, only one solution existed: Flora had to learn French. She firmed her gaze. *Je suis, tu es, il est...*

The words blurred together. Most students didn't commence studying after a full day of service, and Flora swallowed back a yawn. Unfortunately no subject approached music in magnificence, and no subject surpassed French in dullness. Some people lauded the language, expressing a strange enthusiasm for its nasal sounds, but some people also had supported Bonaparte. She concentrated on the words. *Nous sommes, vous êtes, ils sont...*

Music flowed through her, as if inspired by the rhythm of the words. Flora's fingers itched, and she resisted the urge to jot down notes to the melody. That life was over.

She had a new life, one that involved cleaning and sewing and French grammar books. Her life might be unideal, but at least she was alive. There were worse things than French verbs.

A creak sounded, and she stiffened. The softness of the armchair, expertly created by some artisan, did not lessen her sudden discomfort.

Please let no one find me.

Footsteps approached, and before Flora could decide whether she should pretend to be cleaning, even though a lady's maid shouldn't be in this room, a shadow fell over her. Fear prickled her spine, and she braced herself for a chiding from the butler or housekeeper.

Slowly she lifted her gaze.

No scowling upper servant stood before her.

Instead a man attired in gentlemen's clothes arched an eyebrow.

He was tall and imposing and exuded aristocratic charm. Flora's stomach tumbled downward.

The quality of his clothes was impeccable. Flora knew. She'd become an expert in attire. She knew all about mending and sewing and cutting patterns. She knew which fabric lasted, and which didn't.

Flora slammed her book shut. She rose hastily, and the book clattered to the floor with a thud worthy of the most horrendous compilation of subjunctive verbs, lengthy lists of nouns, and headache-inducing grammatical explanations.

"La Grammaire Française," the man read, and his lips curled into a smirk and amusement danced in his dark eyes. "I could have sworn the Duchess of Vernon mentioned you were French."

Fiddle-faddle.

Out of all the people to see her reading, it had to be the Earl of McIntyre, the Duke of Vernon's best friend.

I hope he does not recognize me..

Flora forced her eyelashes down, resisting the urge to peer at him. He was taller than she remembered, and his figure seemed composed of muscular planes. His voice had deepened, though his particular shade of caramel colored hair and the exact shade of brown in his eyes remained the same.

He'd always been handsome, and familiar butterflies settled into her chest, even though the last time butterflies had roamed there, they'd been in Scotland and she'd been seven.

When she dared glance at him again, he was still surveying her with mild amusement.

"You're the first French maid I know who reads French grammar books, lassie," the man said.

"It eez my half day," Flora said hastily, forcing herself to use the French accent she'd adopted when she'd first arrived at the Butterworth vicarage. "I can read anything I like. I wanted to see how they teach French to ze English."

"Ze English?" The earl's eyes twinkled. The man's presence was unnerving.

Confessing was impossible. She rather wished maids were given fans, and not only for their cooling purposes, even though heat surged within her, and their cooling purposes would be welcome. Having an object with which to hide one's face at sudden notice would be magnificent. Instead, she grabbed her feather duster and angled it to obscure her face. "You are most charming, my lord."

He lifted his eyebrows and opened the grammar book. "*Je suis, tu es, il est, elle est, on est, Nous...*" He paused. "Tell me, what comes after?"

"Sommes," she said hastily. "*Naturellment.*"

He put the book down. Thankfully he stopped smirking. "That's correct."

"Of course it is," she said, and her heart sang.

"In my experience the French refrain from pronouncing the 's' at the end. And the word does not contain two syllables."

"Oh." The joy that cascaded through her promptly halted, as if she were a musician who'd played the wrong note and was now subjected to a conductor's glare.

Lord McIntyre's glare seemed sufficiently intimidating.

Flora swallowed hard. She *had* to fix this. If he mentioned this to the duke...

"That's just the—er—accent of my people, *monsieur*. We were not part of ze high society. That's why you must be unfamiliar with it." She forced herself to laugh. "I am flattered I have adjusted so well to this country zat you think me English. I am very proud. You should have heard me when I first arrived."

"I don't believe you," he said flatly. "You're not French."

The words jolted her from her carefully constructed world. She'd heard the words before, but only uttered in nightmares. Her throat dried and she felt faint, as if she were once again witnessing a knife plunging into flesh.

Flora had never considered going on stage, but she'd been pretending to be French for years. No one had doubted her before.

"You're not who you say you are," Lord McIntyre said.

"N-nonsense," Flora stammered. She shifted her legs. The Persian carpet might be more luxurious than anything in the servant's quarters, and it might even be more luxurious than anything in the former house in which she'd worked, but now it brought no comfort.

"You're pretending." The earl fixed his eyes on her, and Flora felt at risk of being mesmerized.

She forced her gaze away quickly, conscious her cheeks seemed to be on fire. The man must have been cavorting with Hephaestus, the Greek god of fire, himself.

Or Hades.

Perhaps the earl had not been referring solely to the god of the underworld when he'd named his gaming hell *Hades' Lair.* Perhaps he'd referred to himself.

Lord McIntyre *knew.*

Her heart adopted a faster rhythm.

She only had to wait until a sufficiently dull break in a conversation, someone else's casual reference to servants, or perhaps to someone venturing onto the subject of deception, for the earl to mention that Flora was not really French and for her whole world to shatter.

It shouldn't have mattered.

She was not the only maid here pretending to be French. Everyone knew women paid French servants more than English ones. French maids were bestowed with all the glamor of Paris, even if they came from remote villages in Brittany.

Flora raised her chin and widened her stance, but the movements did not change the fact that perhaps her falsehood would matter, and the new duchess or her husband would dismiss her.

The earl still held the despised French grammar book in his hands.

"The Duke of Vernon has no fondness for liars." Lord McIntyre's mouth twisted, and Flora was reminded of rumors that Lord McIntyre's father had been a poor guardian to the duke. For a moment the earl was a little boy again, raised beside his father's more lauded charges.

THE EARL'S CHRISTMAS CONSULTANT 9

It didn't matter. Flora and the earl hadn't been close as children, and they certainly wouldn't be now. He hadn't even recognized her.

"Is there something I can help you with?" Flora asked, retaining her French accent.

The earl flushed, perhaps remembering he should not be in the duke's parlor either. "I'll leave. I left an invitation to a Christmas ball on the silver platter by the door."

"Very well, my lord." Flora curtsied.

The earl didn't bother to smile, and there was no kindness in his eyes. He turned and exited the room. The action should have been calming, but her heart raced even after the door to the parlor closed, and it continued to race even after the main door closed.

CHAPTER TWO

WOLFE SCOWLED AND LEFT Callum's townhouse. Since when did he make a habit of conversing with maids? Especially misbehaved ones? It was his own fault for entering Callum's home. At one point he'd spent so much time there his presence in the home had been normal, but that had changed once Callum married Miss Charlotte Butterworth. Everyone knew Callum should have made Wolfe's sister his bride.

Wolfe trudged from the duke's townhouse on Grosvenor Square toward Hades' Lair. He shouldn't have bothered to hand deliver the invitation to Callum. The post was able to move from one section of Mayfair to the other, and early November was an unideal time for a walk. The sky had remained a consistent gray this entire year, but the wind blustered with a far greater force, as if until now it had only been practicing. He clutched the brim of his beaver hat, lest it decide to investigate its capabilities for flight.

The irony of the duke's perpetual absence was not lost on Wolfe. For years he'd urged Callum to relax, to indulge in vices, and finally, Callum had done so spectacularly: breaking off his betrothal with Wolfe's sister and eloping with one of this season's most confirmed bluestockings. Now Callum gallivanted about the capital to attend music performances with his new bride, even though Callum had never shown any interest in music.

Not like Wolfe. Wolfe adored music. Music had been his salvation once, and now it was his solace.

Wolfe was conscious of approving glances from people as he strolled through Mayfair toward Hades' Lair. His attire was impeccable—his valet did a splendid job of maintaining his clothes, despite Wolfe's habit of wandering through London rather than taking a carriage. He sighed, as if exhaling air might also dispel his boredom.

No.

He remained bored.

Finally he ascended the steps to the grand double doors of Hades' Lair. Gargoyles guised as devils grinned at him from their perch on the stone portico. Perhaps Wolfe might never be a research scientist like Lord Somerville or Lord Bowen, but it didn't matter. His gaming hell brought him joy, no matter how often people said it was nothing to be proud of. After all, he employed people. He made people happy. Was it really such a dreadful occupation?

The door opened, and his doorman nodded solemnly. "Good evening, my lord."

"Good evening, Jonas," he said.

Other gaming hells might employ burly guards whose appearance was designed to intimidate, but Wolfe had long learned that intimidating his guests was not conducive to encouraging them to relax sufficiently so that they wagered vast sums. Jonas's skill at oriental fighting methods belied his pleasant appearance. This might be a gaming hell, but he wanted it to serve as his guests' second home. In a world where men married women for mere practicality, second homes were important.

Perhaps Father would have behaved better if he hadn't been living in a remote manor home with a woman to whom he was indifferent, where the only thing he could do was to elevate his status, even by abominable means.

"It's a full crowd tonight," Jonas said.

"Splendid," Wolfe said.

At one point Jonas's words would have brought him pleasure, but Hades' Lair's success was consistent. Many men appreciated a haven of vice to visit, and Wolfe was eager to capitalize on their instinct.

Gambling was not an occupation for the thoughtful. Thought had very little to do with gambling, no matter how much some men might pride themselves on their supposed skills at *vingt-et-un* or whist. The lack of contemplation had always suited Wolfe before. He'd been in the army. He'd killed for years, and contemplation was not something which brought him joy. Quiet was more likely to instill images of death in his mind.

Hades' Lair was a place where men came to be the worst versions of themselves, freed from the observations of their wives, daughters, and in many cases, mistresses. Not all men wanted to discuss politics in the places their parents and grandparents had frequented. Some wanted to gamble and feel the actions of a night still mattered.

"Your sister is in your office," Jonas said.

"Devil it." Wolfe gave Jonas a curt nod, then swept through the gaming hell.

He marched past gentlemen in red armchairs drinking brandy and puffing on cigars as they played cards. The guests were filled with that peculiar confidence of people lauded as youths as the most beloved boys of Eton and Harrow, but who found themselves old and wizened, their silvery manes an imperfect change from the blond tousled curls they'd had when they still wore skeleton and sailor suits.

Music played, its tempo always upbeat, so as to instill exuberance in these men. Energy pulsed unceasingly through Hades' Lair. Festivity was not something relegated to people under thirty-five, and he was happy to create a haven for his guests.

Normally Wolfe enjoyed striding through the gaming hell, but normally his sister was not present. He quickened his steps.

"It's the earl," Sir Seymour shouted merrily from his customary seat, and a few men raised their crystal tumblers.

He murmured a greeting and hurried past. At least the men did not mind he gained money from them. Naturally the promises of more wealth thrust over his guests, but since Wolfe intended to retain money, ultimately those promises would be unfulfilled for most. At least he might give them good drink and music. He did that more successfully than other clubs which prized quiet as a virtue, when it was companionship people craved.

Wolfe knew. He'd grown up in an isolated area, a home filled with three other children, all slightly younger than he was, but all more gifted. The realization he could play a musical instrument had transformed his life and given him the confidence to throw himself in various forms of studies. The fact he could now examine ledgers and manage a large staff brought him constant joy.

Wolfe entered a corridor and then opened the door to his office.

His sister reclined in the leather chair behind his desk. Her long legs were stretched nonchalantly over it, and her immaculately coiffed hair swayed as she turned her head toward him.

"What did I tell you about visiting Hades' Lair?" Wolfe demanded.

Isla rolled her eyes and set her legs onto the floor. "You never used to mind."

"I was lax in my responsibilities as an older brother. No more."

"You're one year older than I am," Isla said. "And I was taller until you were fourteen."

"You've always been exceptionally tall," Wolfe grumbled. "That doesn't negate the fact you shouldn't be here."

"Are you saying your security is not strong?"

"Naturally not," Wolfe said. "It is exceptional. Excellent. Quite ex—"

"Exquisite?" Isla's eyes glimmered. "Jonas does wear a nice uniform."

"I was going for exemplary," Wolfe grumbled.

"I would expect nothing else from you," Isla said in a soothing tone. "Besides, I wanted to surprise you."

"Not a worthy goal."

"I take it I've achieved it," Isla said. "Now sit down. No good having you tower over me, even if you *are* trying to make up for lost time."

Wolfe frowned but he took a seat in the rather less luxurious chair opposite Isla. Despite his irritation at his sister's careless regard for safety, he was happy to see her. "What brings you here?"

"I'm going on a trip. I wanted to say goodbye."

"You're leaving London?"

"I'm leaving Britain." Isla stretched her arms nonchalantly.

Devil it.

Wolfe glanced at the drawer that contained the remaining invitations. "And where exactly are you going?"

"The French Riviera," Isla murmured, as if it were utterly natural for an unmarried woman to declare an intention to visit that cesspool of French immorality.

"I forbid it," Wolfe growled.

His sister's eyes widened in feigned innocence. "But brother dear, the French Riviera will be good for my health."

"Your health is excellent."

"Maintenance, my dear."

"You shouldn't be gallivanting on the continent. You need to marry and be taken care of by someone."

If he'd any doubts in the intelligence of holding a Christmas ball, they vanished. His sister needed to find a new betrothed. The holiday she proposed was dangerous.

"My last engagement hardly went well. I have no desire to while away in some acquaintance's country house."

He sighed. Her broken engagement had left her adrift, but he would solve that. "When do you intend to leave?"

"Next week."

Devil it.

"That's very soon," he remarked.

His sister shrugged. "Perhaps."

"You're an unmarried woman." He forced himself to sound casual. "Whom do you intend to travel with?

"Mrs. Fitzroy," Isla said. "She's married to Admiral Fitzroy, who rather emanates safety. Even though you were in the army, you must be aware of his reputation."

"Naturally," Wolfe admitted, and his shoulders relaxed somewhat. At least his sister had not lost all reason.

From what he knew of Mrs. Fitzroy, the admiral's wife was not prone to such instances of logic. She was far younger than the admiral and was not known for being serious.

Still, Isla was correct. She would be safe under the admiral's care. The man didn't lack money, and his protective instincts were strong and honed by the Royal Navy.

Isla rose and gave him a wide smile. "I will see you for Easter."

He cleared his throat. "You mustn't forget the Christmas ball."

"What Christmas ball?" Isla toppled into her seat.

He strode to his desk, opened a drawer and found her invitation. "Here you go."

She undid the scarlet seal and scanned the contents. "You're arranging a Christmas ball in Scotland?"

"Indeed."

"I haven't been to McIntyre Manor in a long time," she said wistfully.

"Nor have I."

She paused but then shook her head. "Who will attend? People won't want to make the long journey."

"Oh, they will for this," he said confidently, "and we will have the very nicest ball."

"Truly?"

"It's a new tradition," he said blithely. "So it's important you be there for the grand beginning."

She pursed her lips. "But I couldn't possibly travel to the French Riviera and then go to Scotland so quickly. I'll have to join Mrs. Fitzroy *after* Christmas."

"That does seem reasonable," he said lightly.

Isla frowned and reread the invitation. He suppressed the instinct to grin. Isla always did care for festivities. A ball was an occasion for her to select a beautiful dress, look divine and swathe herself in the inevitable praise. And heavens knew, he wanted to give that to her.

Wolfe knew running Hades' Lair only tarnished his sister's reputation. He should have insisted Callum marry Isla earlier, if only so the duke could have come to the realization then that a match with her was impossible.

Perhaps Wolfe could have convinced Callum that whatever Wolfe's father's sins had been, they were none Wolfe desired to repeat himself. It hadn't worked like that, and now Callum was blissfully, happily married to someone else, and Isla was unwed and speaking nonchalantly about crisscrossing the continent.

"We need some traditions," Wolfe said. "You won't want to be with another family for Christmas. It's not the same thing."

"But we never celebrated Christmas."

That was true. In truth, he'd never had much interest in the holiday. His newfound love for it had more to do with its placement in the calendar.

He didn't want to subject his sister to a season. She would be far older than any of the debutantes. *No.* She needed to find a husband soon. Christmas was the time to do it, whether he cared about the holiday or not.

He'd already invited the most eligible bachelors of the *ton*. Anyone who couldn't brave the cold would be automatically discarded, since it didn't bode well for continued visits. There was no point procuring a brother-in-law if it meant he'd lose his sister. He'd invited Callum and his new wife, just so everyone would see Isla was not despondent, no matter what the gossip magazines proclaimed in salacious, fabricated details.

Isla sighed. "I suppose I can consider it."

"You can accept," he said. "You can join Mrs. Fitzroy and her husband in the new year. I know you just want to avoid the season."

She gave a wobbly smile. "Very well. I'll attend."

He grinned. "I'll escort you from here."

His sister stood reluctantly. Wolfe offered her his arm, and his sister took it. They exited the office.

"I didn't know you had such fondness for Christmas." Isla moved her gaze over Hades' Lair, and Wolfe's cheeks warmed. Usually the only emotion Wolfe felt when he saw the place was pride. He may have been raised in an isolated region of Scotland, but the club was never quiet. His guests laughed and gossiped, and every night, Wolfe was richer than he'd been the night before.

For the first time, the constantly flickering candles perched in regularly polished gilt candlesticks seemed...garish. The laughter was at coarse jokes, and the money the customers lost might matter to them. Perhaps he should not feel pride at having created this gaming hell. He didn't want this to be where he met his sister.

She tilted her head and scrutinized him. "I hope you don't intend *me* to organize your Christmas ball."

Devil it.

Wolfe had never hosted a single ball, much less one that contained centuries-old traditions. He knew nothing about Christmas.

"You don't want to? I'd rather hoped you would." Wolfe flashed his most charming smile, but though it worked on debutantes, it was rather less successful on his sister.

"I'll agree to attend, but I have no desire to prolong my visit. I haven't forgotten the cold in Scotland."

"You can showcase your talents at organization."

Her eyes narrowed. "I hope you don't desire to use the ball as an opportunity for me to find another fiancé."

"Er—naturally not. I—er—simply adore the holiday."

"Adore?" She laughed. "What do you even know about Christmas?"

"There's pleasant music and mulled wine and—er—maybe garlands?" His voice rose uncharacteristically as he uttered the last word. He'd never actually attended a Christmas festivity before.

She smirked. "What sort of pleasant music? People will have high expectations. Some of the guests will care about the holiday."

"A surprise, dear sister," he said and assisted her into his coach. He waited until his driver had hooked up the horses and started on the journey to take Isla to his London townhouse.

Wolfe reentered Hades' Lair and called for his secretary.

Isla was correct: a Christmas ball was a large venture, and their parents had never expressed fondness for the holiday, dismissing it as unnecessarily German, just like the current royal family.

Isla had made her disinterest clear, and he wasn't going to plan it himself. What did he know about Christmas?

He needed help. He needed a...Christmas consultant. He'd hire the very best expert in Christmas there was.

"Harrison!" Wolfe shouted.

Harrison soon appeared. "My lord?"

"I would like you to hire a Christmas consultant for me."

The man widened his eyes. "A Christmas consultant, my lord?"

"Indeed."

"Forgive me," his secretary said, "but I am unfamiliar with that occupation. It is possible no such position exists."

"Then we must hope somebody has the skills."

Harrison nodded and left the room.

Wolfe sorted through some sheet music and began to play a song on the piano. The melodic notes distracted him, and he found joy in gliding his fingers over the keys.

CHAPTER THREE

FIDDLE-FADDLE.

Flora had been caught. The duke's friends weren't supposed to enter his townhouse and explore drawing room corners.

But Lord McIntyre had done precisely that, and Flora's carefully constructed identity was demolished. She needed to leave. And certainly her destination *shouldn't* be the Channel Islands. Lord McIntyre had confirmed the paucity of her French skills. If a Scottish earl could discover her lack of language skills in moments, a French person could discover it at once.

She enjoyed working for the duchess, but she couldn't continue to lie, and not just because the duke's best friend was aware of her deception.

Flora glanced at the grandfather clock in the parlor. Mrs. Drakemore's Agency for Good Servants would still be open. She could inquire if she could be placed somewhere else. She'd feel foolish returning, but she would have to inquire.

She inhaled. It would be fine. She was more experienced than before. It would be easy to secure a new position.

It has to be.

Flora spoke to the housekeeper quickly, took her coat, and marched from the townhouse. She pulled her bonnet forward, then strode through Mayfair. London might be her favorite city in the world, but it had also been where her former life had ended. She refused to be discovered.

The air was crisp, and her nostrils constricted. Next month it would be Christmas, but now it was still November and fallen leaves, not snow, crunched beneath her feet. The sky was a gloomy metal color, and it seemed impossible to imagine a season with mistletoe, holly and ivy adorning everything and wassailers strolling from door to door, singing delightful songs.

Finally, Covent Garden in all its glory stretched before her. Crowds huddled around street performers, and a thrill of excitement cascaded through her as she strode past the Theatre Royal. For a moment she could imagine her father still performed there and that everything was fine.

Nothing would be fine again though, and she remembered she couldn't linger. If she were spotted, it would most likely be in this quarter. Mr. Warne enjoyed music, a quality that in no manner redeemed him.

She scanned the crowd, but did not see him. *Good.*

Flora hurried through Covent Garden. The music grew fainter, and she marched over several side streets until she came to the cheerful green building that housed Mrs. Drakemore's Agency for Good Servants.

Street performers and beggars squatted outside, as if to emphasize to any visitors the importance of ensuring one selected someone appropriate, since many in London could be of disreputable character.

She passed through the narrow door. A row of primly dressed people sat in a room decorated with embroidered quotes that glorified the worthiness of work.

THE EARL'S CHRISTMAS CONSULTANT 23

It seemed foolish to be here. She was employed. She might as well be fourteen again, lying about her age and her experience, thankful when Mrs. Drakemore took pity on her and placed her as a maid of all work at a vicarage in rural Norfolk, away from everything she knew, but also away from Mr. Warne.

A clerk sat at a desk, and she approached it. "I would like to speak with Mrs. Drakemore."

"So do many young women."

Flora winced. "I've been employed through her before."

"Ah." The clerk nodded, took her name and instructed her to wait.

Flora settled down with a row of other young women.

Finally the clerk called her name, and Flora was ushered to a large office overlooking the street. Mrs. Drakemore sat at a glossy desk, devoid of papers or books, a testament to the virtues of tidiness.

"Flora Durand," Mrs. Drakemore said. "I was surprised to see your name."

Flora attempted a smile, but it must have wobbled, for Mrs. Drakemore waved her hand dismissively. "Please, take a seat."

Flora did so.

"Now, what brings you here? Does the Duchess of Vernon desire some new servants for her household?"

"You know that I work for her?"

"I make it my business to know everything," Mrs. Drakemore said. "Besides, everyone is talking about how the Duke of Vernon married a daughter of a vicar from Norfolk. I'm delighted things have gone well for you."

Flora's cheeks warmed. "I'm actually not here on behalf of the duchess."

"No?"

She swallowed hard. "I'm here on behalf of myself."

Mrs. Drakemore assessed her. Mrs. Drakemore was a tall, competent woman skilled in mathematics and languages. Mrs. Drakemore could just as easily have managed a boarding school, but she apparently had a preference for the more neatly attired women anxious to become servants, than the spoiled offspring of aristocrats.

"I'm surprised to hear you desire to leave," Mrs. Drakemore said finally. "I would not have thought the duke would be stingy with pay."

"It's not about the money," Flora said.

Mrs. Drakemore's eyebrows rose. "Have you experienced...cruelty?"

"Naturally not."

"Has the advancement of your position been too challenging?"

"No," Flora said. "I simply desire a new challenge. I was hoping for something more...rural."

"You do not care for London?"

"I favor the countryside," Flora said.

The thing was, Flora did like London. She adored London. She'd lived here before, even if she'd told the Butterworth's housekeeper she was new to the capital. London was filled with music. One didn't need to be rich to hear people playing on the streets.

Yet she'd felt safer in Norfolk. The county might be dismissed as dull, but it was also a place people were unlikely to accidentally wander into, a fact that suited Flora fine. Norfolk wasn't on the way to Birmingham or York. She wanted to work in a similar obscure position.

"I will keep you in mind," Mrs. Drakemore said briskly.

"There's nothing available now?" Flora asked. "I'd hoped to start soon."

"You're at a higher position," Mrs. Drakemore said. "I assume you don't want to start over again as a maid of all work?"

Flora wavered, but she supposed Mrs. Drakemore was correct. These things must take time. If Lord McIntyre informed the Duke of Vernon of her deception, she could return to Mrs. Drakemore then to take any position.

"Thank you," Flora said finally. "I suppose I could wait a while longer."

Mrs. Drakemore's eyes softened. "If you can wait, there's a lovely position in Cornwall with a young widowed baroness that starts in late January. I think you would be suited for it. Most of our maids prefer to stay in London."

"That sounds lovely," Flora said.

Cornwall was far from London. She would be unlikely to see Mr. Warne there.

"Good." Mrs. Drakemore scribbled something down. "I will begin arrangements."

Flora thanked Mrs. Drakemore and left her office. It had been too optimistic to hope to acquire something at once. Flora passed the row of potential servants and nodded farewell to the receptionist.

She stepped lightly through the streets and headed toward Covent Garden, musing about Cornwall's secluded beaches and empty countryside. She would be sad to leave the duchess, but Cornwall would be pleasant. She wouldn't have to worry about pretending to be French, and she wouldn't have to worry about being recognized. After all, who went to Cornwall?

Some carolers sang Christmas music, and her heart swelled. The air was crisp, and at some point the sun had set. It didn't matter. Lights sparkled about her.

Normally busy Londoners stopped to observe the carolers.

And then she spotted him.

Mr. Warne.

She hadn't seen him in nearly six years, but it didn't matter. She recognized him.

He was neither particularly tall, nor noticeably short. His waist could be termed normal, and his coloring consisted of brown hair and pale skin, the most common combination in London. Even his age was not of particularly noteworthiness, and she would struggle to describe him to someone else.

And yet, his identity was unmistakable. The exact slope of his nose, his wide jaw which gave his face a pear shaped appearance, featured regularly in her nightmares. Villains never seemed to wear normal buckskin breeches in books, preferring to be clothed in capes and twirling mustaches, but everything about him was normal.

She shivered. Perhaps he chose his clothes with the intent to blend in, like some form of cosmopolitan masquerade. The day before the last day she saw him, she would have only remarked that Mr. Warne was an adequate pianist. But on the last day she'd seen Mr. Warne, he'd been running after her, and ten minutes before that, he'd been murdering her father, the best man in the world.

Flora's heart abandoned its regular rhythm. Terror surged through her. She tried to move to the other side of the road.

Unfortunately, this was Covent Garden at its busiest. People swarmed about her, hindering her ability to cross the street.

She knew she shouldn't look at the man, but had he noticed her? Was he noticing her now? She needed to know.

Carefully she turned her head in his direction, and a moment later his eyes locked with hers.

Perhaps he won't remember me.

Then a cloud drifted over his face, one that did not appear when most people looked at her. His gaze was a strange mixture of glee and fury, the exact sort of compilation one might have if one had murdered someone years ago and now, had spotted the only witness.

Nausea tinged her throat, and her legs felt faint, as if she'd transformed into a Silesian marionette. Her knees buckled.

"Excuse me," a woman said, jostling her, and Flora remembered to walk.

She plodded her legs over the cobblestones. She tried to not remember the man stabbing her father, and she tried to not remember her father's screams, and she tried not to remember staring at her father's limp body, conscious her father's murderer would now want to do the same to her.

She'd spent so much time fleeing and she would need to do so again.

Her heart drummed a crazed rhythm, and she wove through narrow streets until finally she ascertained no one followed her. Tears prickled her eyes.

I have to leave London.

She couldn't wait until the assignment in Cornwall.

Her heart thudded, tangling up with her ability to breathe. If only she'd taken better precautions. She'd felt so hopeful.

Mrs. Drakemore had told her there were no new assignments before January. Could she take on another position and then quit it so soon? Her stomach squeezed. Mrs. Drakemore knew she desired the Cornwall position. She could hardly show up and announce a sudden passion for being a scullery maid.

But perhaps...

An idea occurred to her. If no current positions were available, perhaps she could create her own position. The agency also advertised positions. She only needed to have a position until January. What sort of position would be so short?

The carolers.

Perhaps... She smiled. If there was no assignment for her, she would have to create her own assignment. She knew the *ton*. They always were throwing balls. Perhaps she could call herself a Christmas consultant, for people who didn't want to extend their housekeeper too much.

She could advertise her services. Her father had been Bavarian. He'd taught her all about Christmas. They'd even lived there for a while.

Flora hurried through the streets and back to the duke's and duchess's townhouse. She forced herself to not sprint up the stairs to her room. Once she arrived, she lit a tallow candle, took out a piece of paper and began to write an advert.

Do you desire someone to help you create splendid holiday festivities on your country estate? You need the services of Fräulein Schmidt, an expert in everything Christmas. Fräulein Schmidt comes from Bavaria and is highly knowledgeable about Christmas traditions. She has worked for the British aristocracy for years and plays the piano.

Flora smiled. Tomorrow morning she would give this to Mrs. Drakemore's agency along with the advertising fee.

CHAPTER FOUR

WOLFE ENTERED HADES' Lair. He'd delivered his last invitation, and he hummed a Christmas tune. He strode through the gaming hell and entered his office.

His secretary rose. "I believe I've found a Christmas consultant for you, my lord."

"Magnificent, Harrison."

His secretary was not prone to smiling, perhaps under the impression it was best to devote all his energy solely to assist Wolfe, but on this occasion his lips twitched. "There is an advertisement in *Mrs. Drakemore's Agency for Good Servants* that matches your specifications precisely. May I read the advert?"

"Please do."

Harrison cleared his throat and read a short paragraph lauding a Miss Schmidt's expertise in Christmas and a willingness to work anywhere on the British Isles.

"Good work," Wolfe said. "I never doubted you."

"Thank you." Harrison's eyebrows were perched slightly higher than normal, as if he were also shocked to have procured someone.

"To think you were questioning the authenticity of the position."

"Er—yes," Harrison said, evidently reluctant to mull over his mistake. "I felt it highly unlikely someone would want to travel to Scotland for such a short assignment... Evidently I miscalculated the attractions of Scottish snow and sleet."

"Don't worry, Harrison," Wolfe said lightly. "People say Christmas is magical."

"I hadn't realized the power of Christmas magic."

"I'd thought it a myth as well, equal to stories of centaurs and cyclops." Wolfe grinned. "But after this Christmas, everyone will be aware of its power. I will host the very finest Christmas party."

"Ah," Harrison said.

"Now be sure to answer the advertisement immediately."

"Indeed, my lord." Harrison gave another nod, somehow managing to appear more regal than any of the aristocrats at court, even when he was showing deference. "I will contact this Fräulein Schmidt."

"And after that you must pack my cases. We're going to Scotland now. Immediately."

Harrison's eyes widened, and he dipped into a bow. Wolfe wondered if the servant's sudden lowering of his torso had been to disguise his shock rather than simply as a token of respect.

"I will arrange for a carriage," Harrison said. "I gather you do desire that form of transport? Not the—er—mail coach?"

Harrison's voice was strained, and Wolfe almost smiled. Harrison was not fond of twisting roads in winter, and the cramped mail coach exacerbated his discomfort.

"The carriage will suffice," Wolfe said. "I'm not in so much of a rush to subject us to such unpleasantness. In fact, perhaps you should stay at Hades' Lair in my absence."

Harrison's shoulders relaxed. "Splendid, my lord."

"But let's not tarry," Wolfe continued. "This will be the most wonderful Christmas."

And my sister's reputation will be restored.

"Very good, my lord."

"I would appreciate it if you not mention to anyone that I am hiring someone to assist me," Wolfe said.

"Indeed, my lord?" Harrison's eyebrows rose a fraction of an inch.

"Not just yet. I wouldn't want word to get back to my sister. I implied I would plan everything myself."

"Might I venture to suggest that in that case perhaps you should plan it yourself?"

"Absolutely not. What my sister does not know will not harm her. Just make certain to procure the services of this Fräulein Schmidt."

"I will do so at once," Harrison said.

"Good, good." Wolfe settled back into his chair.

Harrison dutifully left Wolfe, and Callum arrived shortly after.

"I heard you called on me yesterday," Callum said.

"I did," Wolfe replied, somewhat surprised. After his interaction with the maid, he wouldn't have been surprised if she'd taken the invitation he'd left on the silver platter by the door and thrown it in one of the burning fires in the room.

Their interaction had been unideal. He despised people who lied.

For a moment he wondered whether he should inform Callum that his wife's lady's maid was only feigning to be French, but decided against it. It was the sort of thing that could be petty, and from the enthusiastic manner the duchess spoke about her lady's maid, he had the feeling they were close. His status with Callum was still frail after Callum had told him about Wolfe's father's poor treatment of Callum and his twin brother Hamish. Wolfe's father had become Callum's and Hamish's guardian after their parents died, and the twins had lived with Wolfe and Isla for much of their childhood.

"I did call on you," Wolfe said. "It seemed you went to listen to some music?"

Callum's cheeks became a ruddier color. "So I did."

"Our former piano tutor would be most proud of you," Wolfe said.

Callum shrugged. "He wasn't spending time with me at the piano, and you know that."

"No." Wolfe smiled.

Callum and Hamish had consistently impressed their tutors, but Wolfe had always excelled at music. It had been his one skill, until he'd founded Hades' Lair, of course.

"I received your invitation," Callum said.

"Splendid."

"I wasn't aware you liked Christmas."

"Then you thought wrong. Frankly, I adore Christmas."

"You tend to complain when members visit their family during Christmas rather than Hades' Lair."

"That was in the past," Wolfe said matter-of-factly. "And this is the present. The new reformed me likes nothing better than—"

"Roasting chestnuts? Singing yuletide songs? Sitting by the yule log?" Callum suggested.

Wolfe winced. Perhaps it did sound mawkish. He raised his chin anyway. "Yes. I adore all of that. I trust you will join?"

"Are you certain you desire my company? My treatment of your sister was—"

"—atrocious," Wolfe finished for him, and Callum's cheeks took on a darker shade.

"That was in the past," Wolfe said, more gently. "If she can forgive you, I can."

Callum rubbed the back of his neck. "I suppose I could take Charlotte to the Highlands. She still hasn't visited..."

"Splendid. Perhaps you can even host some men in your manor house."

Callum's eyebrows rose.

"I'm trying to matchmake Isla," Wolfe admitted. "Not that you should tell her. These are—"

"—prospects," Callum finished for him. "I see."

"They're all quite well regarded," Wolfe said.

"Perhaps you should let her choose her own prospects," Callum said.

"No one is courting her," Wolfe said.

"Er—right." Callum removed his gaze. "I suppose I damaged her reputation."

"Broken betrothals have a tendency to do that."

"Yes." Callum kept his gaze averted, and he shifted his legs. "I will consult with Charlotte..."

"Splendid." Wolfe clapped his hands together.

With the help of Miss Schmidt, everyone would love the ball and be impressed. He would show everyone his sister came from a good family, despite his work at Hades' Lair, and someone would propose to her.

CHAPTER FIVE

THE KITCHEN BUSTLED with movement, and Flora glanced at the door, waiting for a sign the post had arrived. Someone needed to answer her advert.

"You're spending a good deal of time in the kitchen," the housekeeper remarked.

Flora squared her shoulders. "There is an abundance of mending to do, and the light is better in the kitchen."

"Ah." The housekeeper dropped her gaze to Flora's sewing. "I don't see any holes in those clothes."

"A stitch in time saves nine," Flora said.

It would have been more convenient if the duchess had torn her attire. If there was a letter for Flora, she wanted to read it. It was probable the other servants might not assume mail directed to Miss Schmidt was meant for her. She'd used the first German name she'd thought of. At least she wouldn't be feigning expertise in a new language this time.

Finally, the mail arrived, and Flora rushed to it with the enthusiasm of a person waiting for a letter from a loved one abroad.

There was a letter.

Her name was written in faultless curves, and Flora's heartbeat quickened. The quality of the paper was evident, and Flora unfolded the paper quickly, lest someone spot the false surname.

Someone wanted her to be a Christmas consultant in Scotland. She reread the letter twice, but she hadn't mistaken the contents. She wanted to scream with delight.

Scotland.

It had worked.

Someone had hired her.

She would be a Christmas consultant in Scotland, and then she would travel to Cornwall to work for the widowed baroness. Mrs. Drakemore did not even know Flora was the Miss Schmidt who'd placed the ad.

Thank goodness for Christmas.

She'd loved the season before, but now it had saved her.

The letter instructed her to correspond with a Mr. Harrison. The employer, it seemed, desired to be anonymous, but that was fine. People might appreciate discretion. Everyone knew people hired scullery and chamber maids, but the *ton* might not like to admit they needed to pay for help for Christmas. Perhaps some widower with children was flummoxed by the approaching holiday or perhaps a new bride simply wanted advice for her first ball.

Flora's heart sang.

Not only would Flora be able to be a Christmas consultant, but she would be one in the Highlands. No region on this island was farther from London. It made even Cornwall appear close.

Christmas was the very loveliest holiday.

The thought of returning to the Highlands sent butterflies twirling and dancing through her body, as if contemplating the possibility of lifting her there by sheer exuberance.

Flora clutched the letter in her hand. It denoted hope and impending happiness.

And *leaving*.

Her mouth dried. She'd loved working for the Duchess of Vernon. They were almost the same age, and she'd assisted the duchess and her sister before they'd married, when they'd still been dismissed as vicar's daughters.

She gathered the duchess's garments.

The housekeeper raised her eyebrows. "You finished mending all of them."

"Indeed," Flora said smoothly, before sweeping past her and carrying the clothes to the duchess's chambers. She moved briskly up the winding servant's staircase and then pushed open the door to enter the far grander corridor that led to the duke's and duchess's chambers.

She knocked on the duchess's door and entered.

"Flora," the duchess said.

"Your Grace."

The duchess scrunched her nose, and her pince-nez wobbled. "It's odd to have you call me that."

"Things have changed," Flora said.

"I suppose."

Flora surveyed the room. It faced Grosvenor Square and golden light spilled through the windows. The duchess's bed was always immaculately made, a testament to the frequency with which the duchess spent the night in the duke's room. Everything in the room seemed to sparkle.

Flora set down the basket of garments, conscious her fingers were wobbling.

"Do you have a moment?" she asked.

The duchess nodded, but her eyebrows rose slightly. Flora shivered, aware of the other woman's intelligence.

"I'm afraid I must resign," Flora said rapidly, as if the speed in which she said it could make the duchess forget about the meaning of the words, could make *Flora* forget about the words' meaning.

"Truly?" the duchess asked.

Flora nodded. "I do love it here, but I-I just can't be here longer."

"Oh." The duchess drew back.

"You'd rather work for someone else than me?" the duchess asked.

"Yes," Flora said.

The answer did not seem to be the right one. Her mistress appeared crestfallen.

"I mean, of course I would rather work with you," Flora said hastily. "But not—"

"In Guernsey," the duchess finished.

"*Precisement.*"

The duchess tilted her head, and appeared thoughtful. "And you don't much like London."

"No." Flora shook her head, glad that at least this was not a lie.

At one time she'd adored London. But that had changed once her father was murdered. But the duchess did not need to know that.

When she'd taken on a position with the Butterworths, she'd done so because they'd lived in a hamlet in Norfolk. She'd felt safe working in the vicarage. Mr. Butterworth was a good man, and she'd been happy to attend to his wife and two daughters. She'd felt at times uncomfortable maintaining the charade of being a Frenchwoman, but she'd been concerned for her safety.

Mr. Warne was a powerful man. He was much admired in society. Everyone had marveled at the rapidity with which Mr. Warne had made his fortune, even though he'd been only the third son of a viscount, and even though the wars on the continent had been raging, and even those not battling overseas struggled. She had no doubt people would rather continue to believe in Mr. Warne's magnificence than her.

She sighed. Her father had simply tutored Mr. Warne in piano, and she still wasn't certain why that would cause Mr. Warne to murder him.

"I've already found a new position," Flora said, returning her attention to the duchess. "I would like to start immediately. If you can do without me."

"I will miss you very much," the duchess said.

"I'm sorry." Flora felt her lips tremble. She'd expected this conversation to be difficult, but it was proving even more so. She would miss the duchess. "I'm so grateful for everything you did."

"Where will you go?"

"I found a placement in Cornwall," Flora said.

"I see," the duchess was silent for a moment. "You are always welcome to call on me. I consider you a friend. If something is troubling you, you can tell me."

Flora's breath caught. This was the moment when she could confess. Yet how could she? Mr. Warne was too dangerous, and Flora would be safe soon.

"If you decide you would like to return here after all," the duchess continued, "I am certain I can find something."

"Thank you," Flora said. "You are very kind."

They spoke for a few more minutes, reminiscing about their time in Norfolk. Flora might be the duchess's maid, but they'd always been close. The duchess was quieter than the rest of her family, and Flora had felt drawn to her. Now the duchess no longer needed her.

The afternoon passed quickly. Flora was conscious each task would be her last.

The next day she took a hack to Smithfield Market. People filled the square, and she clutched her bag to her, conscious it held her compositions. She might not have access to a piano, but she could still compose music. She'd done so ever since her father had first taught her.

Though the mail coach appeared luxurious from the street, Flora knew no luxury could mask the hundreds of uncomfortable miles until Scotland, not improved by the late month. She used the ticket she'd procured from Mr. Harrison and boarded the mail coach. She sat near a large family with sniffling children who seemed entranced in a novel game of seeing if their coughing could mask the ever grinding wheels, though they remained unsuccessful.

Am I mad to do this?

Scotland was her past, and she'd avoided her past successfully until now.

She shook her head. Scotland was not where The Event had happened. That had been in London. That had been where her whole world had changed and everything had vanished forever.

Flora was so accustomed to working, suddenly not working was almost a shock to her. She didn't need to sew anything, she didn't need to press anything, and she didn't need to do any of the hundred other tasks she was accustomed to doing.

There was only sitting on a coach with strangers, and there was only thinking about what would happen when she arrived there. She wished Harrison had given her the name of her new employer, and Flora forced away a prickle of worry.

Music ran through her head, perhaps inspired by the climbing ascent of the wheels as they ground over the occasional stone, rocking in a new, ever changing rhythm as they rounded an increased number of curves.

It will be fine. It will be wonderful. It will be...Christmas.

She tried to grasp onto the melody that rushed through her heart, holding it close, memorizing it for when she might take ink to some paper and jot down the notes and hold onto them forever.

It was better to concentrate on the music that surged through her than on the man she'd seen in Covent Garden.

CHAPTER SIX

HARRISON'S EFFICIENCY extended to the final day of the journey. A carriage had picked her up at her last posting inn stop, and Flora settled into the conveyance, appreciating the added comfort now she was not surrounded by other people.

She took a tiny nap, but was woken by the swaying of the carriage as it climbed a long hill. Her stomach tightened uncomfortably, and she opened the curtains to the carriage.

In the distance was the ocean, and before it were dark brown hills, speckled with snow. Foamy gray waves crashed against the shore, and gusts of wind ruffled the few shrubs. Snowflakes started to fall, and she smiled. Snow made everything better. Snow was crisp and clean, and it blanketed the ground, wiping away any imperfections, any mud, any unsightly ditches.

This was her chance to live again in the place of her youth, when life had been as close to perfect as it ever would be. She'd been seven when she'd left the Highlands, and she tried to remember what the manor home had looked like. The memories that flitted through her mind were confined to her father's happiness, the delight of frolicking through fields, and memories of a handsome boy with dark eyes and a serious face.

This place resembled that of her memories. The trees were similar and even the curves in the road were similar.

THE EARL'S CHRISTMAS CONSULTANT 43

Is the landscape too *familiar?*

She couldn't be far from McIntyre Manor. She tried to think about which other aristocrats lived in the area. Would they know her?

Surely not. Most likely she was being foolish. Perhaps the manor house belonged to Lord Hamish Montgomery, the duke's twin brother. She may have seen him when she'd been frequenting the Butterworth home before, but he'd never recognized her.

Would he recognize her now?

His wife would.

Lady Hamish Montgomery was the duchess's older sister.

She did not want to explain to Lady Hamish Montgomery why she was here, and why she was not a French maid.

She inhaled. Most likely she was nowhere near McIntyre Manor. The area might appear familiar, but she'd been a child then. What did she know about the landscape?

Finally, a manor home came into view. The building was cold and spare and unwelcoming, and she told herself this could not be the same place she remembered. The fact that she shivered had nothing to do with premonition.

It only meant it was chilly.

But there was something about the manor house... The stern gray form, not softened by the gables on the otherwise mostly flat roof, seemed familiar.

Nonsense. Lord McIntyre was hardly the type to care about Christmas. Christmas had nothing to do with gaming hells.

There had to be other, equally grand houses in this region with occupants who had not mocked her during the previous week.

It's the manor house.

Fiddle-faddle.

She couldn't appear at Lord McIntyre's manor home and announce herself as Fräulein Schmidt, Christmas consultant. That would be absolute nonsense.

She had to leave. *Now.*

She craned her neck from the window. "Driver! Driver! Please stop."

The man did so, surprise evident in his expression.

"I need to return," she said.

The coach driver raised his eyebrows. "I can't do that, Miss."

"It's important," she pleaded.

The coach driver chuckled. "We're almost here."

Indeed, the coach wheels crunched against gravel, and the snowflakes fell from the sky with greater force.

Oh, no. Oh, no. Oh, no.

Her heart clenched, and she smoothed her dress frantically, as if less sharp creases might make her appearance more tolerable for the earl. There'd been a time when she'd adored McIntyre Manor. Many times she'd longed to be back, remembering its idyllic grounds.

Nothing about returning here would be pleasant now.

The coach stopped, and even though she should be grateful for the halt to the coach's interminable swaying, she wasn't.

The coach driver opened the door. "It's really not so bad here, fräulein."

"It's not that," she said, but he strode past her and began hauling her belongings from the coach.

A woman in a dark gown and a murky cloak stepped from a small door. "Welcome to McIntyre Manor, Fräulein Schmidt. I'm Mrs. Potter, the housekeeper."

The woman had a friendly smile and warm eyes that twinkled.

"Th-thank you, Mrs. Potter."

"I trust you had a pleasant drive?"

"Y-yes," Flora stammered.

"She enjoyed it so much she wanted me to take her straight back down," the coach driver declared. "Ain't many people that like those curves."

"The views *are* pretty," the housekeeper said.

"They are," Flora admitted, feeling guilty her primary emotion had been queasiness before it had been replaced with fear.

"Now let's get you a nice cup of tea," the housekeeper said. "You must be exhausted, poor thing."

"Practically delirious," the coach driver said, but his voice was kind, and Flora's heart ached.

They were good people. It would be nice to work with them.

"This way Fräulein Schmidt," the housekeeper said. "The earl will see you."

A shiver descended down Flora's spine.

CHAPTER SEVEN

WOLFE STRODE MERRILY down the corridor of McIntyre Manor. His heart thrummed a festive tune.

He was finally going to meet Fräulein Schmidt.

He stepped into the parlor. The room was perhaps an unconventional place for him to have meetings, but the wood-paneled study would always remind him of his father. The parlor was light and bright, seeming to capture even the dullest amount of sun with efficiency.

A woman was sitting on the sofa. *This must be her.* She had dark hair and a round face that reminded him of someone, and he lengthened his strides.

Until he stopped.

The woman looked curiously like someone he knew, someone he couldn't *quite* place.

Wolfe didn't know any Germans. The only German he'd ever known had been his former piano tutor, but that had been ages ago.

"Fräulein Schmidt?" he asked.

The woman turned to him, perhaps conscious of his gaze, and Wolfe's nostrils flared.

What was the Duchess of Vernon's lady's maid doing in his library in Scotland? And why did the servants tell him Fräulein Schmidt had arrived?

Had *she* written the advertisement? Had she simply sought a new identity after he'd discovered her deception of posing as a French maid? Anger surged through him.

He'd thought he'd hired a professional.

Wolfe's nostrils flared. "Or should I say *Flora*? I was not aware the Duchess of Vernon had traveled hundreds of miles to see me with her lady's maid. Or did you decide to come on your own?"

The woman's face paled. Well, that was a start. She should feel ashamed.

"Do you just go about the country lying about your identity?" he asked.

She shook her head violently.

"Are you mocking me?" he asked.

She widened her eyes.

Damnation. He'd wanted to give Isla the perfect Christmas. He could send Harrison to find someone else, but by that time whomever was the replacement would have no time to actually do the job.

"Do you know what you've done?" Wolfe asked.

The woman was irritatingly silent.

He stepped closer to her. "You've ruined Christmas."

She inhaled.

The woman looked upset. What on earth did she think would happen by coming here of all places?

But then he remembered Harrison had found her advertisement. *Devil it.* She was probably as horrified to see him as he was. The only problem was he *knew* who she was. She was a woman who'd until recently been solely concerned with her mistress's hair and attire. He didn't need someone with passable skills in sewing. He needed a Christmas consultant.

Footsteps sounded behind him. His housekeeper approached them, carrying a tray. "I've brought some tea up for you both."

"Now is not the time," Wolfe said, striving to sound polite.

"It's always the right time for tea, my lord," Mrs. Potter said with a smile. "I have some shortbread too."

Shortbread.

He wrinkled his nose, but he couldn't fight the pleasant aroma emitting from the silver tray his housekeeper clutched. The shortbread looked enticing.

"I suppose you can put it down," he said brusquely. "No point you carrying it all the way down to the kitchen again."

"No, my lord," Mrs. Potter said, though she appeared somewhat befuddled.

He swallowed hard. Even his housekeeper had noticed how excited he'd been to have a Christmas consultant. He'd made a point of telling them to be *nice* to the new employee. As if the housekeeper and her staff weren't already naturally nice.

Flora took the teapot. "How do you take your tea, my lord?"

"Black," he said.

"With quite a bit of milk and sugar," the housekeeper said. "The earl does have a sweet tooth. He was always raiding the sugar here as a child."

"I wasn't the only one doing that," Wolfe grumbled.

"Have a shortbread," the housekeeper said.

"It's not necessary."

"My lord." The housekeeper fixed a stern gaze on him, as if she still remembered him as a child and thought he was of immediate need of growing. Evidently no amount of muscle or inches had dissuaded her from that opinion.

Wolfe took one dutifully. "Er—thank you."

The housekeeper beamed.

Flora poured herself some tea, though he noticed she did not take quite as much as she'd poured for him and she'd added no sugar.

He frowned and pushed the sugar toward her. There was no point in drinking tea without adding all the other delicious things one could add to it.

"If I'd thought you were the person whom Harrison represented, I never would have come here," Flora said, once the housekeeper left.

"I already invited people," Wolfe said. "I sent them invitations promising the most lavish Christmas ball in Britain. And now I'm to have some...maid arrange it?"

Flora stiffened. "I'm a lady's maid to a duchess."

"Does she know you're here?"

"No," Flora admitted. "But I gave my notice. I have a new position in January in Cornwall and wanted something before then."

"I see." The duke inhaled. "It doesn't matter. We both know the duke's bride was never supposed to become a duchess. Vernon didn't marry her for her beauty and style."

"The duke is very happy."

Wolfe stiffened. He did not care to be reminded that Callum did not regret breaking his engagement with Isla.

"My lord," Flora said, and her voice was softer. "I assure you I do have all the skills necessary for a Christmas consultant."

"You mean to say you're intimately familiar with Bavarian holiday traditions? Perhaps you even speak German?" Wolfe smirked. "You also said you spoke French. And your skills were abominable."

Flora's cheeks pinkened.

"Did you come here to ridicule me?" Wolfe asked.

"What? No. Of course not. I had no idea you would be here," she said quickly. "Harrison said the person in question wanted his identity to be secret."

Wolfe groaned. He had. Having someone organize a Christmas party was the sort of thing that could make other people in the *ton* laugh. It was the sort of thing people said wives could be helpful for. He didn't need matchmaking mamas to thrust their daughters at him with even greater glee than they were doing now, and he certainly did not want anyone to know how bad a job he was doing at helping his sister.

"What do you even know about Christmas?" Wolfe asked.

"Many things."

"You lied."

"Not in the advertisement," she said truthfully. "I can do the job," she said.

"You're not Bavarian."

"I am," she countered. "At least, my father was."

He gave her a hard stare, but she didn't waver.

"You might think I lied," Flora said, raising her chin, "but I assure you I did not."

"You mean you didn't want to be caught," Wolfe grumbled.

Wolfe thought about the other people in his house. He didn't know Christmas, and he was certain the housekeeper and Harrison, brilliant as they both were, could not be asked to plan a festivity. He'd wanted to rival the very best balls of the *ton*.

"And why exactly should I keep you?" he asked.

"I don't want you to keep me," Flora said. "I want to leave. Immediately."

"Then why don't you?" He fixed narrowed eyes at her.

"I-I tried to, but the coach driver laughed at me. He—er—thought I was jesting. And I didn't recognize the location until it was too late."

"Oh." The earl frowned. "*Recognize?*"

CHAPTER EIGHT

FLORA SHRANK BACK.

"This is the Highlands, lassie. You shouldn't be recognizing anything here."

"Of course not. I used the wrong word."

Please let him believe that. Please. Please. Please.

Emotions fluttered through her body, causing her heart to tip and totter against her ribs.

He continued to assess her. "Have you been here before?"

She wavered.

"Don't lie to me again."

"I—" She relaxed her shoulders.

He's not Mr. Warne. Whatever he was—angry, handsome, he had not murdered her father. He'd even *liked* her father.

She inhaled deeply. "My father worked here for a while."

"Indeed? And what nationality was he?"

"Bavarian."

The earl blinked. His eyes remained on her, as if assessing whether she resembled her bearded father.

"Bavarian?" he asked softly. "Then you're—"

She nodded. "I'm Greta. Greta Braun."

His eyes widened.

"You didn't forget me?" she asked.

He shook his head, and a flurry of emotions danced in his eyes.

"You can't be," he said finally, and his features hardened. "You have a habit of lying. You must have heard somehow I had a music tutor with a daughter. I won't believe you." His chest puffed out. "I refuse to believe you."

"It's true," she said softly. "And I'm not lying. I-I didn't want to tell you, remember? If I were trying to trick you, I wouldn't be posing here as a Miss Schmidt."

He was silent, perhaps contemplating the logic of her statement. "The girl I remember had dark hair like you and hazel eyes like you."

She blinked. Most people assumed her eyes were brown.

"But the girl I remember couldn't have been older than six—"

"I was seven when I left," she said.

"The fact remains that is not enough to convince me."

"Then what should I do?" She stared at him. "Tell you everything I remember about the household?"

He winced. "Follow me. I have a method to solve this quickly."

A prickle of nervousness went through her, but she followed him. The walk was short, and he gestured to a grand piano. It was magnificent, and she inhaled.

"Play something," he demanded.

She walked slowly to the glossy piano. "It's so beautiful."

"Yes," he said proudly.

The Duke of Vernon had a piano in his townhouse, but music was never a passion of his and the piano sat against the wall. This was a grand piano. A Broadwood.

"The Greta I knew played the piano sweetly."

"I didn't know you listened to me."

He flushed. "There should be some sheet music here." He opened a box and placed something before her.

"Are you testing my ability to read music?"

"I just want to know you can play." He gave a wry smile. "Most servants wouldn't know how to."

She hesitated. "Then I will play my own piece."

His eyes widened.

Perhaps she'd confessed too much. No one knew she composed her own music. But when would she have another chance to play music on such a lovely piano?

"Very well," he said.

"I haven't played in a while," she warned him.

"If you play at all you will be special."

She nodded and glanced at the piano. The black and white keys were enticing, and the rest of it was all sleek wooden curves. "Let me fetch my music."

"Hurry."

She rushed up the steps to the room the housekeeper had allotted for her. Most likely she would have to leave it soon. Even if the earl believed her, that didn't mean he desired her to stay. She grabbed her compositions, hurried down the steps and slid onto the piano seat. The keys glistened temptingly before her.

Her body shook, but something in her heart still sang. She was going to play the piano.

"Go ahead."

"N-naturally." Flora was jolted from her musings. "It's just so beautiful."

The earl raised his eyebrows, and she inhaled.

And in the next moment she was playing. She played the melody she'd composed during her trip, when she'd had emotions whirling through her. And then she played other melodies, composed at the vicarage, at the Butterworth's London town home and finally in the capital. She concentrated on the sounds of the keys, losing herself in the music. For a moment she could pretend this was her piano, and that everything in the world was wonderful.

She didn't want to glance at the earl. She didn't want to see his expression. Would he believe her? Would he still despise her even if he did?

All that mattered now was the piano and her music.

Finally, she stopped.

WOLFE HADN'T EXPECTED to enjoy the music. The music had been a test. One he was feeling rapidly guilty about.

Some women excelled at music. Music, like watercolors or sewing, was a feminine pursuit, and this woman did it with aplomb.

Music was something one needed to be taught, and in Wolfe's experience, masters did not go about giving lessons to maids. This woman seemed to have been taught. Her fingers had flown over the keys. She'd given each note the correct weight, the correct length.

"You're Herr Braun's daughter," Wolfe said.

She nodded.

"I should have believed you. I'm sorry. I just didn't—"

"—expect me," she finished. "I know."

He nodded. "I think I have to take a seat."

She gave a wobbly smile.

"You needn't play more," he said. "Though that was...beautiful."

"Thank you."

"Your father was the finest tutor I ever had. Had it not been for him..." He shook his head. "I'm happy to have met you. How is your father?"

She stiffened. "He's dead."

His heart squeezed.

Before Herr Braun had shown any interest in him, Wolfe had been called hopeless. Isla was younger than Wolfe, but she'd learned to read far more quickly, as had Callum and Hamish. He'd been conscious of attempting to learn, but whatever techniques for learning had worked so easily with Isla, never worked with him.

His tutors had berated him with unrelenting frequency, scolding him. His mother had looked at him with disappointment, and his father had not veiled any of his horror at the inability of Wolfe to do something they all deemed simple.

But reading? Reading had seemed impossible.

Isla had been able to spend hours turning pages of books, speaking of castles and princesses, dragons and sea voyages, with glee, but for him it had just been paper with black squiggles on it until the music teacher had arrived.

Obviously he'd not come to teach piano to Wolfe. Wolfe had needed to focus on his lessons after all. Even though the piano was respected, it was not respected over reading or doing arithmetic.

But Herr Braun had been able to make the most glorious sounds from the piano that sat untouched in the parlor, and after he'd left, Wolfe had gathered up his courage to sit on the piano bench and play the keys himself. He'd only needed to observe the piano tutor. That had been all to repeat the rhythm that he'd played.

On some occasions Wolfe wondered what might have happened to him if the piano tutor had never noticed Wolfe playing and had never taken it upon himself to teach Wolfe. The man had been the very first one to offer Wolfe encouragement, and it had been the first time Wolfe had been truly good at something that didn't consist of running or wrestling, but of something with Wolfe's mind.

It meant Wolfe was not simply strong, but that he had some intelligence.

It had been enough.

It had been the hope his parents had needed, but more importantly it had been the hope he himself had needed. After that, Wolfe was not simply dismissed as the idiot son. He was no longer termed a disgrace to his ancestors. He'd learned so many songs on the piano, moving on to other instruments. He'd always been adept at using his hands, but this time what he created could was termed beautiful.

And this was the daughter of that man?

Vaguely he remembered a little girl with dark hair, shyly observing him.

"I suppose Callum does not know your identity either?" he asked.

"I was worried he might remember, but he never did. It was good."

There was something about the way she said 'good,' that made him think it was anything but.

She'd been coming to his house for years as a child, and yet he had not recognized her. He'd seen only the dark plain clothes that all maids wore, and dismissed her as someone whose life had nothing to do with his own.

His stomach hurt.

She smiled. "You needn't look so guilty."

"I don't look guilty," he protested, but she only laughed.

WOLFE STARED AWKWARDLY at his newest servant. "I suppose I should call you Greta."

"Oh, no," she said quickly. "Miss Schmidt is fine. Or Flora even. That's what the duchess called me."

"You don't want to remember your old life?"

Flora averted her eyes, and a wave of suspicion rose through him. What sort of secrets did this woman have?

This wasn't the Christmas consultant he'd desired. She was far too young, and too slender to denote appropriate jolliness.

They would be in the manor house for a month together. He'd been imagining a fussy older woman.

Flora was...appealing.

The woman was pretty. She wasn't supposed to be pretty, and he wasn't supposed to notice.

Unfortunately he very much did notice.

"You are—er—welcome to play the piano while you are here."

"Thank you, my lord. I may stay?"

"There's no other option," he said curtly, and hurt seemed to appear on her face.

Never mind.

She'd lied.

Was her father even dead? Why were her relatives permitting her to work as a maid? Her father had been a court performer. He could hardly have died penniless.

There was something she was not telling him, and he didn't care to discover what it was.

"Very well," she said and continued to play the piano.

He considered apologizing, but she was playing so beautifully. He didn't want to interrupt her. He would only make her uncomfortable.

He tiptoed back up the stairs, remembering why he always preferred London. The noise from the streets could sometimes mask his thoughts, and the never ending work at Hades' Lair could distract him during the daytime.

He didn't need to remember then that he was the little boy whom his father had always scolded, who had always done things wrong, just by being.

Devil it.

It had been a mistake to try to organize a Christmas ball here. If only he could cancel the ball, but he knew that was impossible. By the time any message from him would arrive, the guests would already be beginning their long journey here. He should have let Isla go to France and he could have spent his time in Hades' Lair, just as he did every year.

CHAPTER NINE

NORMALLY HARRISON WOKE him in the morning, but a noise interrupted Wolfe's slumber. He rubbed his eyes for a moment, taking in his new surroundings.

McIntyre Mansion.

He was in his boyhood room. He hadn't wanted to take his father's former room, even though that was the largest one. Isla could stay there when she arrived.

It was sufficiently disconcerting to be in the same room he'd had as a child. The familiar tartan blankets were draped over the same heavy dark furniture. The same landscape paintings graced the same green wallpapered walls.

Something sounded again outside.

How late had he slept?

He rose from his bed, grabbed his robe and put it on, and then stepped onto his balcony. Snow covered the hills. Gusts, even colder than normal, brushed against him. He tied his robe more tightly about him, and then he saw her.

It was...Flora.

She was stepping into a carriage. Where on earth was she going?

But only one thought was in his mind: away.

Was this because of him? Had he made her leave?

Obviously.

He'd behaved abominably toward her. Forcing her to play the piano like some animal at the zoo.

That hadn't been his intention. He'd been angry at her, but where would she go? Maids weren't known to possess an abundance of funds.

And Scotland was no place for someone without money.

Her figure was small, and he gazed at the road and the billows of snow. Evidently she'd convinced one of the grooms to give her a ride on a carriage, and his nostrils flared.

She shouldn't be leaving.

"Wait!" he hollered, but his voice was swallowed by the wind. *Devil it.*

"George, George," he called out quickly.

His valet came rushing through the adjoining room. "My lord?"

"I need to get dressed. At once."

His valet blinked. "Very well, my lord."

"Make the clothes warm. And simple. Not too many buttons." He gazed out at Flora's retreating form.

The valet's lips quirked up, and Wolfe suppressed a groan.

If he were smart, he would just stay inside and read his paper and make some general comments to his valet if he got too bored about the state of the world and how it had not improved as much as it could have, but evidently he was not sensible.

Once his valet helped him dress, Wolfe rushed out to his butler and demanded to know where Flora had gone.

"I must confess I am not entirely certain," the butler said. "I could ask the housekeeper though."

"Never mind."

Wolfe rushed outside. The cold air whipped about him. No one seemed to think it was terribly urgent that Flora was leaving. *No matter.* He was going to bring her back.

He'd been too harsh yesterday. Scotland had its charms, but like any part of the British Isles, he would hardly advocate Flora explore it on her own. The idea would be preposterous. Was she even sufficiently rested after her long journey? She obviously was not thinking correctly if she was leaving.

He sprinted toward the stables, not caring that he was covering himself in snow.

He ordered a surprised groom to prepare a sleigh. If she was leaving, she most likely needed to catch the coach in the next town.

Even though the sleigh was prepared hastily, by the time the horses were attached to it, the carriage with Flora was gone.

"Where to?" the driver asked. "Do you want to visit the lake? The ice is frozen."

"No, no," Wolfe said. "The nearest town. Take me there."

"Very well, my lord," the driver said solemnly. If he was surprised, he did not show it. Wolfe could not remember the last time he'd gone to the neighboring town.

Soon the sleigh seemed to fly over the snow. Cold wind whipped into Wolfe's face, but he didn't care. He just needed to get to Flora. He needed to apologize. He'd treated her dreadfully last night.

Flora's father shouldn't have died without any plans. Flora's father had been one of the foremost piano tutors in all of Britain. Wolfe knew. His father had boasted on it often. He would hardly have been destitute.

Wolfe would have expected Flora to become a governess or a teacher. She was intelligent. She played piano brilliantly, and he didn't want to imagine how well she might play if she had more access to a piano. She shouldn't be a mere maid.

Perhaps her position had risen with the duke's new wife's, but Wolfe knew the Butterworth family. They were kind people, but of decidedly modest means. Any service job with them would have lacked glamor.

What exactly had happened to her?

Finally, the sleigh entered the town.

"Where would you like to go?" the driver asked. "The public house has an excellent mulled wine."

"Nonsense. I'm looking for a girl."

The driver's eyebrows rose.

"She has brown hair and is pretty with a heart-shaped face and a turned up nose."

"You must really like her," the driver said kindly.

"What? Nonsense," Wolfe blustered. "She just happens to be pretty. That's all."

The driver nodded, but Wolfe had the horrible impression he hadn't entirely convinced him.

Never mind.

It was a fact.

Flora *was* pretty. Any idiot could tell that.

"Is that her?" the driver said, pointing to a woman.

Wolfe could only see her profile from his position in the sleigh, but he recognized her immediately.

"Yes, that's her."

The driver stopped and Wolfe hopped from the sleigh.

"Should I wait for you?" the driver asked.

"Yes, yes. Get yourself a drink," Wolfe shouted.

The driver beamed. "I do love Christmas."

Wolfe bounded over the road.

"Wait," Wolfe hollered to Flora. "Don't go."

Flora turned around.

He'd found her.

Wolfe allowed himself to grin.

Snow fluttered downward, landing on her hat, her cape and even the wisps of dark hair that peeked from her brim and curled enticingly.

"What are you doing here, my lord?" Flora asked. Her eyes were wide, and she stepped back, a fact he despised.

"I'm stopping you from leaving," he declared.

"My lord?"

He swallowed hard. "I was unfair yesterday." He frowned. "Perhaps not precisely unfair, but I should not have made you feel you had to leave."

"You worry about the expense?"

"It is sizeable," Wolfe said.

"Indeed." The woman nodded gravely. "But I am not going to London."

"No?"

A soft smile played upon her lips. "I am going shopping."

He blinked.

"I am very grateful for everything your servants have procured, but there is more to do. Your housekeeper assured me I could order on your credit."

"Oh." Wolfe felt his cheeks warm. He cleared his throat. "What do you desire to purchase?"

"First I intend to go the haberdashery."

"You desire to buy ribbons for your dress."

She smiled. "There are many other uses for ribbons. I would like ribbons tied on each candelabra. Emerald green and ruby red, the colors of Christmas."

"I see," he said.

"And then I would like to procure some spices. Cloves and however many oranges are available. I also have a list of drinks I would like to serve."

"Oh." Wolfe felt foolish he'd rushed out of his home so quickly. He should have just talked to one of his servants.

"And lastly," she said, "we'll need more candles. I was also hoping to find some musicians that will be able to play for us."

"My father used to employ some locals. I can give you their information."

"Wonderful. They will need to play Christmas music. I have brought sheet music they can use to practice."

"Oh. That is very good."

"I thought so," she said. "I assure you, my lord, you will have an excellent, most magnificent Christmas. It's the very loveliest holiday of them all."

"Hmph." Wolfe glanced toward The Lamb's Inn, where his driver was undoubtedly regaling himself. Wolfe was reluctant to leave so soon. "I suppose I could accompany you…"

She raised her eyebrows.

He shrugged. "I must admit to some curiosity on the wonders of Christmas."

"I don't remember your family celebrating it," she said quietly.

He shook his head, and she gave him a soft smile that made him blush. She'd likely seen just how little regard his parents had had for him. It was something he tended to keep quiet from women, particularly pretty ones.

Not that he would put her in that category. After all, she was simply a servant, not a potential wife or even a potential bed companion for a single night.

"The streets are more filled than I remember them," Wolfe said.

"Mm—hmm. It's quite hard work to be a commoner."

His cheeks heated again, and he glanced in the direction of the haberdashery. Women entered and exited it, carrying packages.

"Let us not linger," he said.

"Very well, my lord."

They entered the store, and he was the only man inside the shop. About twenty different women crowded around the small room, and a few people's eyes widened when they saw him.

Jeweled and pastel colored fabric lay in interesting spools. Rich velvet, glossy satin and silk, more practical linen and cotton, and lace and floral patterns lay beside one another.

"You must think this is quite dull," Flora said.

"I've never been in this sort of store before."

"Oh." Her eyes sparkled. "Welcomed to a haberdashery. I suppose ribbons are never an important part of your costume."

He smiled.

They moved from shop to shop, their arms filled with bags. Finally, they finished. Snowflakes tumbled down, and the wind quickened. The wind's strength was formidable.

"My knowledge of shopping is limited," Wolfe said, "but I do know that public house. According to my driver, they serve an excellent mulled wine there."

"I've never had a mulled wine before," Flora said.

"Then follow me," Wolfe said, leading them to the gray stone building.

CHAPTER TEN

THE EARL OPENED THE door to the public house, and Flora stepped inside. The scent of ale and meat pies wafted through the room, and men and women chatted over narrow wooden tables piled high with food. Some of them had parcels tucked underneath. The people's faces were ruddy, as if warmed by their drinks. The large fire that danced in the hearth undoubtedly had warming powers as well, and when she glanced at her cloak, the snowflakes that had fallen on it were already disappearing.

Flora's sole experience of public houses was from traveling. She associated them with an enclosed space filled with grumpy men, all equally irritated by the hassles of the journey, attempting to quell their boredom with drink, but only succeeding in creating boorish behavior. This place seemed imbued with a greater charm. Someone even played a violin. A piano sat unused in the corner of the room, its top adorned with greenery. The grey granite walls might appear sober in another tavern, but the plentitude of candles and their accompanying flickering candlelight rendered everything cheerful.

The earl turned to her and gave her a reassuring smile, as if they were children again in the nearby forest and he was ascertaining she'd made it over an imposing fallen trunk. He then spoke to the barmaid, who led them to a narrow table.

Flora's cloak and the earl's greatcoat were whisked away, and the earl helped her into a seat, as if it were completely normal for them to dine together.

Perhaps it was not entirely appropriate for her to be alone with the earl.

No. This was different. It would not be appropriate for an unmarried woman who was a member of the *ton* to be alone with him, but she was a servant, and the rules were different. They were there for convenience's sake, and that was it.

"We don't have to be here," she said.

"Of course we do," he said. "I want to apologize for my behavior last night. I was surprised. You played beautifully."

"Thank you."

"You are very talented," he said, and warmth flew to Flora's cheeks.

"I enjoyed it," she admitted. "In the end."

"I suppose you don't often play before audiences," the earl mused.

"Indeed not."

He leaned back, and his attire tightened around his chest. Flora averted her eyes. He'd evidently dressed hastily, for he'd seemed to have selected a too small waistcoat. The broad width of his chest was assuredly evident. He hadn't shaved this morning, and dark strands of hair prickled his face, imbuing him with an added masculinity that was entirely unnecessary. The man was already an Adonis.

Butterflies invaded Flora's chest. Ever since she'd met the earl again, they'd developed a decidedly annoying habit of flapping their invisible wings at the most inopportune times and robbing her of knowing what to say.

Her fingers trembled, and she shoved them on her lap and attempted to smile.

"This is nice," she squeaked.

The earl was a kind man, even if he did run a gaming hell, a venue not traditionally known for its adherence to virtue.

After a short while, the barmaid came and placed drinks before them.

Flora leaned forward and inhaled the ruby colored drink.

"It's mulled wine," the earl said. "Perfect for Christmas."

"Oh."

The earl shrugged, but his lips were already spreading into a smile. "I know some things about the holiday." He picked up his tankard, and they clinked.

The barmaid brought food to the table.

"It's delicious," Flora remarked, biting into a meat pie.

"I'm glad." The earl leaned forward conspiratorially. "It's the first time I'm here."

"I suppose this is not near London."

"Indeed not."

"They've decorated it nicely for the holiday," Flora remarked, observing the evergreen boughs and other greenery.

It was better to scrutinize her surroundings than the man before her. One thing had been when they'd been shopping, and she could concentrate on her shopping tasks, but quite another was to sit across from him, as if they were a proper couple.

"The wonderful thing about Christmas is that all of the garlands have meanings," she said quickly, seizing on something to say, though not quite comfortable with her pedantic topic.

"Is that so?" the earl's eyes shone.

"Yes," Flora squeaked.

He gazed around the room. He seemed to hesitate and then he pointed to some greenery hanging from a low beam. "I see this often. What is it?"

Warmth surged over her cheeks. "That's mistletoe."

Mistletoe was common at this time of year, but somehow in his presence, her voice wobbled. She almost looked away. "Servants have a tradition of kissing beneath it. It is supposed to be bad luck to refuse a kiss."

"Ah. How very romantic."

"Mm...hmm," she said, and her heart squeezed. Discussing this with him differed from discussing it with anyone else. It was the sort of conversation that made her wonder what it would be like to kiss...him.

The room seemed to grow more still, and it took a moment for her to realize that the violinist had simply stopped playing, and that not all the world had stopped.

A man approached the table. Flora had seen him behind the bar and she imagined this was the publican. The man bowed. "It is a pleasure to have you here, my lord."

"My lord?" The man from the table beside them looked up. "Is that the earl?"

"It is indeed," the publican said. "Isn't it?" his voice wobbled as if he weren't entirely certain.

"I'm Lord McIntyre," the earl said.

"Taking the missus to our pub," the other man beamed. "There's not anything like The Lamb's Inn."

Flora's cheeks heated again. The man thought them married. She didn't want to look at Wolfe.

"I hardly think he would take a countess 'ere," another man said.

"Of course he would," the first man declared. "Ain't nothing nicer."

The earl cleared his throat. "Though this woman is beautiful *and* refined, she is not my wife."

"Yet," another man called out, and the room laughed.

"She's working on creating a Christmas ball," the earl said.

"Ah, my very favorite holiday," the publican said.

Wolfe's eyes glimmered, and he leaned toward Flora. "Why don't you play some Christmas music on the piano?"

"I couldn't," she said.

"Why not? It will be fun. And I've heard you play."

Playing before an audience. That would be a novel experience. That was something she'd avoided.

But this was not London. This would not get back to anyone. And it would be pleasant, just once, to perform.

She rose, and the earl smiled.

She didn't want to contemplate how easy it was to go along with his suggestions, how nice it was to make him smile.

"Ladies and gentlemen," the earl said, "may I present the wonderful Miss—"

She gave him a strained look.

"Miss Schmidt, bringing you a Christmas collection."

The people in the public house clapped politely.

Flora's heart soared, and she smiled at his excessive display. She sat down at the piano, removed her gloves and stared down at the keys, conscious of two dozen eyes staring at her. And then, with a flourish, she began to play.

She chose a light song. The men started to sing the notes. Their deep voices lacked polish, and they knew the choruses far better than the rest of the verses, but it didn't matter. It was amusing, and she tried to remember the last time she'd experienced such amusement.

Her fingers pranced over the black and white keys, and her heart sang.

After she finished the song, a shadow fell over the piano keys. She gazed up. The earl stood before her. "Mind if I join you?"

"Naturally not," she said.

He sat beside her, and even though his leg did not touch hers, she was aware of it.

She frowned. One wasn't supposed to retain childhood fancies decades later.

"Do you know The Twelve Days of Christmas?" The earl's voice rumbled in her ear.

She nodded.

"I'll play the accompanying part," he said.

They played together, and for the first time in a long time, she felt not nearly as alone.

Finally, the driver appeared, and Flora knew it was time to leave. The earl must have spoken to him before he joined her. At some point the packages had been swept up, and she wondered how long they'd been playing. The earl did not seem to mind.

Flora and the earl stood, and the crowd in the public house applauded.

Flora curtsied, and the earl swept into a deep bow.

"I was happy to have that moment," she said.

"A woman who plays as well as you do requires an audience," the earl said.

"Once that was my dream too," she said, and the earl looked curiously at her.

The Christmas melodies continued to course through her body as they left the public house. The snow had halted, and the earl helped her into the sleigh. He sat beside her and tucked them into a thick woolen blanket.

Then the sleigh moved through the village. Stone houses were on either side of her, and in the distance was the ocean.

"It's beautiful here," she murmured.

"Yes."

"You should spend more time here."

"Perhaps."

"I suppose you must be missing London and your...business."

"The gaming hell?" The earl grinned. "It will manage without me."

The sleigh moved from the village, and the earl took on a pensive expression. "I do wonder what things would have been like if my father had been more warm-hearted."

The earl was being kind. Flora remembered the late earl. He'd never even approached being warm-hearted.

"Not all fathers are fatherly," she said gently.

"Some of that was my fault."

"Your fault?" she exclaimed.

"It took me so long to learn how to read. That's why learning to play the piano was so important to me."

"Oh."

The earl turned to her. "I think of your father often. Everything would be quite different if I never had his influence."

"Truly?"

He nodded, his face grave. "He was the first person to believe in me."

She had a strange instinct to squeeze his hand. Doing so would be improper, more improper than anything else today, and instead she returned her gaze to the landscape. "He always spoke highly of you."

"I'm glad," he said.

She wouldn't have been able to speak about her father even if somebody had inquired about him. Most people assumed him to be absent, perhaps a victim of the war, or perhaps simply a victim of alcohol or a deadly spout of influenza. It wasn't uncommon for people to not have known their fathers at all.

But she'd known her father. And he'd been wonderful.

Her breath caught, as she remembered how suddenly it had all ended. She tried to emanate a veneer of calm. One thing was informing the earl her father was dead, and quite another was informing him how.

It was suddenly important to speak about anything else. She glanced about her. She spotted the frozen lake in the distance.

"You used to ice skate on that lake," she said.

"I did," the earl said. "You remembered."

"I always wished I could go too," she confessed.

"You were too little," he said.

She narrowed her eyes. "That's debatable."

"Ice skating is a proper sport," he announced. "Far more difficult than walking. How could you ice skate if you'd only mastered walking a few years before?"

"I'm sure I could have," Flora said.

They spoke more about ice skating, and she was relieved the conversation had turned to a far safer topic, even if the earl was now in the process of cataloguing the injuries he and his friends had received from skating, and how they'd never even scraped a knee from similar actions on the ground.

CHAPTER ELEVEN

THE SUN SEEMED TO HAVE decided not to make an appearance today, and clouds covered the sky, but Wolfe did not care. Yesterday had been surprisingly pleasant, even if his valet had scolded him for the speed with which he'd dressed, and Wolfe was similarly enthusiastic about today.

The breakfast, certainly, was good. Wolfe took another bite of his turtulong biscuit.

A servant opened the door with a tray of more of Cook's sugary delights. Music drifted into the room.

"Is that Miss Schmidt?" he asked.

"Oh, yes." The maid smiled. "She does play beautifully."

"Indeed," he agreed, and for a moment he sat in placid contentment. The snow had stopped falling, and it reclined in graceful slopes outside the windows, still visible despite the frost-covered panes.

"She should have some biscuits too." He rose and picked up the tray, absentmindedly noting the swift upward movement of the maid's eyebrows.

No matter.

He strode from the room toward the parlor.

Playing music with Flora yesterday had been impulsive, but it had been delightful. Even visiting shops had been amusing. Wolfe had gone shopping before, but only during a specifically arranged time when the store was closed to all other people. He was far more experienced at visiting taverns, though normally he would be whisked to a private room once the proprietors either recognized him or noted the always impeccable carriage. He'd never taken a lady to a tavern before: it would be inappropriate.

But Flora was his employee, and at one time she'd been his friend. The rules were different. She wasn't a married woman who required discretion and whose tastes were expensive, even though they'd never earned money.

He rounded the corner, past the heavy wooden furniture of his ancestors, and the music became stronger.

The sound was beautiful, melodic, and it seemed to wrap about Wolfe's heart and squeeze it.

He entered the parlor and moved gingerly toward a settee, careful not to make a noise, lest Flora stop. It seemed vital she not stop playing. She played most delightfully, even if he didn't recognize the music. Perhaps it was some new continental composer. Ever since Handel had come to England a century ago, gifted musicians flocked to London. It was one of the things he liked most about living there.

Flora's face was round, and she had full cheeks he had a strange urge to caress. Her hair was dark, and her skin pale. He supposed maids did not have much opportunity to go outside. Her hair was tied into a neat bun. Nothing about her was particularly remarkable, and yet his heart tightened in her presence.

He'd didn't recognize the music she played. Perhaps it was the same composer she'd selected on her first day. A strange splurge of jealousy moved through him that he tried to push away. Most likely she was simply playing some Bavarian composer with wizened skin and a steep stoop everyone knew.

Yet Wolfe prided himself on his knowledge of music. He delighted in visiting concert halls. He often chose pianists to play in Hades' Lair.

"You play beautifully," Wolfe said. "What is it?"

She smiled, and her eyes sparkled. "A piece by an unknown composer."

He hesitated. He would have said more, but he didn't want to be overly complimentary of another man's compositions. Perhaps thoughts of this man made her eyes take on a dreamy appearance. "Your playing was the nicest part." He beamed, conscious he had said the right thing.

For some reason Flora did not beam in a similar manner. The woman should know a compliment. Her smile wobbled, and she glanced down at her fingers. Wolfe followed her gaze, and noted absentmindedly that her fingers were long, slender, and utterly elegant. He drew his gaze up.

"I made some mistakes when I was playing," Flora said.

"It's all about practice."

She nodded. "Sometimes I played piano when no one was home at the vicarage, but the Butterworths didn't have a piano in London."

"The Duke of Vernon has a piano," Wolfe mused. "Though if I know the duke, he probably never bothered to tune it."

Flora giggled. "He never liked to practice."

"You remember?"

She nodded.

"How the man thought reading centuries old scientific treaties was more interesting, is still beyond me," Wolfe said.

"I'm sure though he would have let you play. Especially if you had reminded him of your true identity. You are talented."

Flora looked down. "I never asked."

"Oh." Wolfe blinked. Flora seemed so passionate about music. "Why didn't you?"

"It's not important," she said, but he had the impression it was important. She didn't meet his eyes, and her gaze drifted to the tray of biscuits.

"Would you like one?" He offered her the tray.

"Those are supposed to be for Christmas."

"The maid brought them up to me."

"Probably because they were cooling in the kitchen," Flora said. "Do you like them?"

"They're delicious," he said.

"Then I'll make more."

"I didn't hire you to be a cook," he said.

"And Christmas biscuits are an important part. Your cook told me she hadn't even planned to make a Christmas cake."

"Well, surely there's time..."

"It's supposed to be made a month in advance," Flora said. "I'd hoped the biscuits could distract people."

"Don't forget the mulled wine."

Flora giggled, and Wolfe wanted it to be because she remembered yesterday.

"So this composer," Wolfe said tentatively. "Is it the same person you played when I first met you?"

Her smile broadened. "Indeed. In fact...I wrote it."

"Truly?"

Flora smiled. "You needn't look that surprised."

"Oh, no." He scratched the back of his neck and attempted to muster a look of utter calm.

"Are you surprised because I'm a woman?" she asked.

"Naturally not," he insisted. "But music is a whole language of its own."

She shrugged. "Yes. You could say that."

"And you're a—er—"

"A servant," she said.

He nodded.

"I am," she said. "I wasn't always though," she said softly.

"Naturally. I'm sorry."

She'd been playing merrily before he came into the room.

"Forgive me," he said. "I'm simply astounded. But I don't understand... Why would you keep it secret?"

"I would rather not talk about it," she said, and Wolfe narrowed his eyes.

That would not do.

CHAPTER TWELVE

"THAT'S IT," WOLFE SAID. "We're going outside."

Flora was not allowed to appear sad. He clasped her hand and pulled her from the piano seat. He shivered slightly, though that was likely because of the slight coolness of her fingers.

Not the narrow distance between them and the view it provided of succulent lips and large hazel eyes.

Naturally not.

He dropped hold of her hand, but forced a smile on his face and vowed to cheer her up.

"Where are we going?" she asked.

"That's not important," he said, frantically thinking of a place she might find amusing. "The important thing is that we are going to have a good time."

She blinked, and then her lips spread into a smile that made him certain he was doing the correct thing, even if he'd already spent the entire last day with her and he was fairly certain most people would not deem it appropriate to spend so much time with one's female staff.

"The past is behind us, but right now, a good time is imminently possible," he declared.

"Oh?"

THE EARL'S CHRISTMAS CONSULTANT 83

He nodded. "I'm sure there are more things I can teach you about Christmas."

"You didn't even know about the magic of mistletoe," Flora protested.

Wolfe smirked. "That's true."

Flora narrowed her eyes, as if not quite believing him. That was because she was clever. Of course he knew about the wonders of mistletoe. He'd known back in Eton about it, and perhaps on reflection, that's why he was eager to have his sister meet someone at Christmas. The holiday was rumored to be magical, even if he'd never seen any evidence.

"Put on your coat and boots," he said.

"Oh?" She raised her eyebrows.

"And then follow me," he announced.

"Just where do you plan to take me?"

"Not far," he said. "We won't even take a sleigh."

"I suppose you desire to admire the grandeur of the home from the other side. Because I've already seen it."

"I know, silly thing," he said.

She flushed, perhaps at the familiarity, and the back of his neck warmed.

"Come on," he said, ushering her outside. "I just need to speak to a footman."

She frowned. "Are you certain this is not your method of flinging me from the house?"

"Nonsense." He grinned and then moved quickly downstairs. He wasn't going to wait for a footman to answer a bell. He had an idea for where to take her, and it was wonderful.

He soon procured a bag from the footman and slung it over his shoulder. Flora didn't need to see the contents. Not yet at least.

They left the manor house.

Flora started toward the stables, but he grabbed her hand.

"This way," he said.

"But there's no road..."

"What's a few inches?"

For a moment her eyes widened, and then she giggled.

They moved over the snow. Their gait became more awkward, and he clasped onto her hand, lest she fall. Falling was the sort of activity that might lead to her catching a cold, and he had no intention of getting her sick. He wondered how her father had died.

They rounded the house, and then he led them toward the clustering of trees. Beyond the trees was the woodman's cottage, and beyond that, was the lake, which his valet had mentioned was frozen and which the downstairs staff had confirmed.

"You're taking us to the lake?" Flora's voice wobbled, and she glanced uncertainly at him.

"I'm taking us ice skating," Wolfe declared.

"But I don't know how—"

"I'll teach you," Wolfe said nonchalantly. "I believe you mentioned an interest."

Her cheeks pinkened. "That was years ago."

"It doesn't matter."

He hadn't been skating for years. Wolfe inhaled the crisp, clean air. The sky was gray, but it no longer snowed. Evidently yesterday's snowfall had sufficed.

Finally, they came to the clearing through the trees. Hills sloped in the background, but it was the glassy center Wolfe pointed at.

"Some of the servant boys went this morning. It should be quite firm."

"Oh. It's beautiful."

He grinned. "Come on. Let's go."

She drew back. "I don't have skates..."

"I've brought my sister's," he said, removing glossy white ice skates from his bag.

She drew back. "Would she like that?"

"She's not here," he said. "Besides, I remember you being friends."

"That was a long time ago," Flora said.

Wolfe shrugged and led her to a stone bench some ancestor had had placed there. He gestured for her to sit and then knelt on the snow. It crunched beneath him, but he only smiled at her.

"I'll help you."

"I'm a lady's maid," she said. "I'm aware of the process of putting on boots."

"The trick is to tighten the laces," he said authoritatively.

He helped her slide her feet from her boots. He leaned nearer her, close enough for them to kiss, a thought that should not occur to him and sent butterflies fluttering through him all the same. Her feet were small, even when swathed in thick woolen socks, and he averted his eyes, lest he linger on the sight of her ankle.

"Perhaps you should do them after all," he said, and his voice sounded hoarse in his ears.

Wolfe was accustomed to being surrounded by women who frequented the finest Parisian dressmakers, who wore dresses that highlighted their cleavage in vibrant colors that enhanced their coloring. Flora's hair didn't gleam like gold and her cloak could hardly have been termed anything but basic. And yet, at that moment, he wasn't certain he'd ever seen a prettier sight.

Dark tendrils peeked from her woolen hat, and her skin was flushed from the cold. She shivered slightly, and he hastily put on his ice skates. He then took her hand. Their fingers didn't touch: they both wore mittens. And yet some emotion seemed to rush through him anyway, some fire that warmed him and made him uneasy in the cold.

It wasn't possible that he...cared for her.

Wolfe wondered whether he should curse the inconvenience. One wasn't supposed to ponder the perfections of one's servants. And yet Flora wasn't just a servant, and a strange hopeful feeling seemed to flutter in his chest. It was the same feeling that made him think of pulling her into his arms, and the same feeling that made him think of kissing her.

He swallowed hard and reminded himself she was only here briefly. After Christmas ended, she would go to Cornwall, far from Scotland, far even from London, and he would never see her again. Earls did not call upon women who worked as companions to widows in Cornwall, and something in his heart panged.

He shook his head, as if the action would dissipate his sudden sentimentality. After all he was, what else was he supposed to do with himself now? It was perfectly natural for him to want to spend time with her. No guests had arrived yet, and it was important he monitor her progress, and that they discuss details.

He didn't desire to dwell on the fact that inviting her to go ice skating could be described as distracting her and that they could not very well install an ice pond in the ballroom for the guests to enjoy.

Skating with her now was purely pleasure, even though it involved excessive layers of attire and the risk of falling on slippery ice. He hadn't intended to go skating with her this morning, but he was happy he'd invited her. Ice skating always cheered him up. It would be pleasant to focus on something besides ledgers.

He grasped her hand firmly and strode toward the pond.

"I don't think I'll be very good," she warned him.

"It will be fun. I promise." He turned to her. "But if you don't like it at any point, you can simply tell me and we'll stop."

She smiled hesitantly and moved tentatively over the snow. He offered her his hand and she took it.

He hadn't realized that teaching someone ice skating necessarily involved holding their hand, and something in his heart ached, like a note of warning. Finally, her legs seemed to straighten and her shoulders moved back, and she flashed a smile at him.

They wobbled as they walked through the snow on their skates and then he stepped onto the ice. He smiled, enjoying the new texture of the ice beneath him. He'd forgotten just how much fun he'd had with this. He glided over the ice and then returned to help Flora onto it.

She stepped tentatively onto it and then stopped. "It's slippery."

"That's the point."

"But it's *very* slippery."

"I won't let anything happen to you," he promised, not certain if he was only speaking about the ice.

She inhaled. "Very well. I suppose I could try." She extended her hand to him, and he helped Flora all the way onto the ice.

He clasped her hand on his. She tightened her grip, and his stomach lurched. He inhaled, willing away the strange flutters in his heart, and guided her. Her legs were stiff, as if she'd locked them.

"I can't move anywhere," she said sternly. "It's impossible."

He grinned. "Not impossible."

She craned her neck down to inspect her skates. "I'm sure there must be a better way to construct these."

"They work fine. You just have to bend your knees slightly and move your feet to the right and left."

THE MAN WAS IMPOSSIBLE. He seemed to think skating easy.

Flora inhaled the crisp air and gazed at her surroundings. The manor house was barely visible through the trees. Hills jutted up around the lake.

Flora stumbled, and for a horrible moment, she thought she would fall. It would not be the most dignified manner to behave before an earl. "I think people are supposed to learn skating when they're younger."

"I don't know," Wolfe said. "I think I'm enjoying it this way. I find this much more amusing."

"Because I'm a taller person now and am more likely to have a more dramatic fall?"

"No, that's not the reason." She looked down at her hand. His hand was over hers.

She shivered and she thought it was not entirely because of the cold. This was about him. The thought thundered in her mind. She should not have found herself outside. Skating was a sport, but it had differed from any other she had known.

The butterflies that had fluttered through her body when she was five years old descended now, despite the frigid temperature.

"I should have invited you when we were children," he said more seriously.

She shook her head. "I would have been too shy to say anything."

She directed her attention back to her skates. "Are you certain there is something amusing about this, or is the only amusement seeing other people fall?"

"Why would you say that?"

"Because I think it quite likely that I will fall soon."

"You haven't moved."

"Standing here is actually quite difficult. I would appreciate a tree to hang onto."

"I'm not a tree." Wolfe smiled. "But you can take my hand, and I assure you it will be less painful than if you fall."

"I suppose there's some veracity in that statement."

"Come," Wolfe said. "We'll proceed slowly."

"Exceedingly slowly."

"My preferred pace."

"Very well." Flora inched one skate forward and then slowly moved the other one to match it.

She took some steps tentatively on the ice.

"Good job," he said, his voice full of encouragement.

She laughed. "You're enjoying this."

He shrugged. "Perhaps. I'm glad to have something to teach you, since you're giving your Christmas expertise."

"I should never have mentioned that I hadn't been ice skating before."

"You're sure you're not enjoying this?"

She sighed. She was enjoying this. More than was proper. Her heart felt full.

"Excellent," Wolfe said. "I can already see your talent."

"Nonsense."

Wolfe smiled. It seemed nice that they were smiling again.

"I'm sorry I lied," Flora said, and her tone was more serious.

"You didn't lie," Wolfe said. "That was your business. You created the advert, and we answered it. Though perhaps I should ask Harrison to do more thorough checks in the future. We were perhaps so eager to secure your services that we may have been a bit lax."

"You don't mind I'm not what you expected?"

"I don't mind at all."

Flora's feet wobbled. For a moment she'd forgotten she was on skates, but Wolfe put his hands around her waist and steadied her. She was aware of just how tall the man was, and she tilted her head up so as to see all of him.

His eyes were kind. They'd been kind even when he was younger. He brushed away a lock of her hair. "Now you can see better." Then he rearranged her hat.

Flora's heart thundered in her chest. The gesture shouldn't have meant so much. He was just being gentlemanly.

And yet she was aware even in the wind of his masculine scent that sent more flutters through her body. She glanced up at his profile, noting his chiseled features.

He was older than before, but it was him. It was Wolfe, no matter how nicely he dressed himself now, no matter that this whole place was now his.

Longing rushed through her. His eyes seemed to soften, and then even though she was certain he was much taller than she was, his lips moved toward her.

Was he going to kiss her? Was she closing the distance? Was he reading her mind? It seemed like he was narrowing the distance.

The thought was ridiculous. They were of such different classes. Her heart shouldn't be thudding in her chest as if the world might change. Even though she'd thought she'd mastered the art of skating, for some reason even standing on her skates seemed risky, and her knees threatened to buckle.

She averted her eyes, not because she didn't want to look, to see the gold rim around the green irises, but because she didn't want to be foolish. If she saw tenderness there, it must be her imagination, or it must be simply the tenderness a kind man might have for a wounded animal.

And then she fell.

Inelegantly.

"Fiddle-faddle," she said.

The moment was broken.

"I let go of your hand," Wolfe said apologetically. "It was my fault."

"You were arranging my hat."

"Yes."

They didn't mention what else it seemed he was doing. Perhaps it was her imagination. It had to be her imagination. After all, he was an earl, and she was his servant. He was handsome and brilliant, and any lady would be happy to have him.

He probably had had many women in his life. Women who didn't spend their days working and their nights tucked into attics, sharing beds with other servant girls.

And yet her heart still thudded.

"Perhaps we should return," she said.

"Yes," he said. "We've done standing. That's excellent progress. We can move to skating another time."

"I did move that inch."

"Yes," he said merrily. "Yes. You've gone skating. I should go back too. I have much work to do."

"Truly? You brought work with you."

"Yes," he said, though he didn't quite meet her eyes. "After all, I run a very large, very prestigious organization. I have much to do."

"Naturally," she said, and she was once again aware of the disparities between them. She must have imagined the almost kiss.

She wasn't prone to imagining things, but surely it must be something that would occur to everyone, sometime.

Or perhaps it was simply the power of Christmas, that made even the most unlikely things seem possible. Perhaps not all Christmas magic was good.

She turned her head sharply. "Those trees look quite interesting."

"Well, they look like the other trees," he said. "But yes, they are interesting, I suppose."

His tone was all politeness, but she refused to blush.

"I thought we could use it as a Christmas tree."

He blinked. "What on earth is that?"

"The royals have it."

"I did not know you were acquainted with the whims of the royals."

"Well, I am acquainted with the whims of Germans, and it was popular in Bavaria to bring trees indoors and decorate them."

"I see. The regent also favors making his pavilion look like the Taj Mahal, but that doesn't mean we have to do that."

"I didn't know you were so fond of his pavilion."

His face blushed.

"I'm not here to discuss the finer architectural details of the pavilion," she said.

"Why on earth would people want to bring trees indoors?" he asked.

She swallowed hard, for a moment not quite sure why it was so very popular to bring Christmas trees indoors. Perhaps it was an odd notion. Perhaps he was correct to be skeptical.

"The tree will survive with just a bit of water," she said. "If we can find a way to prop it up, it will be quite pleasant to look at, and we can hang all sort of baubles on it."

"I'm not sure I'm convinced."

"You don't have to be. You're paying me to know what to do."

His face definitely seemed to be ruddier.

"Now, do you know where to find an ax, or should I find your woodman?"

He cleared his throat. "You may ask the housekeeper for help in locating the woodman tomorrow morning and instruct him on which tree to cut."

She blinked. "Of course. You're quite busy."

"Yes," he said curtly.

THE DAY HAD TURNED awkward, and he lengthened his strides. The snow crunched beneath them, sounding awkwardly into the air. How had he come from suggesting skating to almost kissing her?

He quickened his strides to the manor house.

He'd had such an urge to kiss her. If she hadn't fallen, he would have. He could still imagine how her lips might taste, how it might feel to run his hands through her hair and he could still remember how it felt to clasp her dainty waist in his hands.

He couldn't go about kissing her. She worked for him. The thought of kissing her was preposterous.

He was not going to be one of *those* men. He'd thought he would ask her to dine with him. Her position was different from that of a mere maid. Sometimes he dined with Harrison, but now Harrison was away, still finalizing things at Hades' Lair. Dining alone wasn't something he embraced, and they still had a lot to talk about. It would practically be a business meeting.

And yet... He turned to her. All that he thought about was the shape of her small nose, the smoothness of her cheeks, and the manner they had pinkened because of the frosty temperature.

When they returned to the manor house, he did not invite her to dine with him.

CHAPTER THIRTEEN

I SHOULD HAVE ASKED her to dine with me.

He'd felt bound by a propriety he hadn't known he subscribed to.

Since when had she become so beautiful? She'd seemed ordinary in London, a poor testament to his powers of observation. Now he was conscious of the particular energy she brought and recognized it as improper. The night before though they'd dined at the public house together.

The following afternoon, when he next saw her, he did not hesitate to speak with Flora. "Have dinner with me."

"Truly?"

"I don't have anyone else to have dinner with," he said hastily. "Besides, we can make it a business meeting. You can tell me about your ideas for the ball, and we can see how we can have it."

She nodded. "Very well."

AN ADVANTAGE OF NOT having many clothes was that Flora did not have to worry about what to wear. She chose her nicest dress, the one she'd planned to wear at the ball. Not that she would be dancing. She would be speaking with the servants and making certain the ball was going smoothly.

She washed first, and then she took off her morning dress and slipped on her best dress. It was a respectable black, though the color had long ago faded. In certain lights it appeared blue, and in others brown. It would have to do. She placed a lace collar around her neck that she hoped improved it, and then she swept her hair up into a knot.

Her hair appeared harsh, and she frowned. Perhaps she could do something more elegant. She always wore a stern knot, but she knew how to do many hairstyles. Perhaps she could do one on herself.

She borrowed some curling tongs. She was unused to using them at this angle, but she found the procedure somehow relaxing. It was nice to have something else to concentrate on, and she smiled when she saw herself in the mirror.

She should be thinking about the food, that promised to be more delicious than anything she encountered in the servants' quarter, but the thoughts in her mind were not of the food, but of dining with the earl.

Finally, she entered the dining room.

The man was handsome, unnervingly so. Candlelight imbued the room with a warmth she did not associate with the manor house. She wondered what it would look like when the candelabras also had Christmas decorations. There wasn't any music, and it was just them, but it still seemed wonderful.

The earl appeared regal. He seemed more somber, and his smile was less wide than before. He'd also dressed for dinner, even though she was just a servant, and surely it would not have been strictly necessary. Silver cufflinks gleamed under the candlelight.

WHEN WOLFE SAW HER enter the room, he knew dinner was a bad idea after all. It had seemed to make sense at the time. He had wanted to prolong the joy of the day, and they did, after all, need to talk. Why not when they were eating?

It was a simple practicality. A mathematical solution.

And yet, nothing about her reminded him of mathematics. She was beautiful. She'd worn a different gown, though equally plain, embellished by a simple lace collar around her neck that made his chest tighten. He considered whether it had been expensive for her. It might be nice to buy her something beautiful. He imagined visiting the haberdashery, but rather than selecting ribbons for candelabras and chandeliers, they would select ribbons for her.

Her hair was arranged beautifully. No earrings, no necklace, and no fan obscured her. She didn't sparkle by other means, but solely by some light within her. It was odd that he'd had dinners with dozens of beautiful women over the years, often in his private apartments, and yet he wasn't sure they affected him in the same manner as she did.

He jumped to his feet, conscious he'd been too late in greeting her, lost in his own thoughts. He helped her into a seat. Something flickered on the footman's face, but then the food arrived.

The food was probably delicious, but he couldn't taste it. The only thing he concentrated on was Flora herself. She appeared beautiful.

He directed the conversation to the Christmas ball, lest he continue to compliment her. Such a thing might cause even the most stalwart footman to raise his eyebrow. He was having dinner, that was all.

"Why are you hosting the Christmas ball?" Flora asked after a while.

"You think it unusual for an unmarried man?"

"I wasn't dwelling on the fact that you were unmarried," she said.

"My sister is also unmarried," he said. "My friend, the Duke of Vernon, was supposed to marry her. But she ran off with—"

"My mistress," Flora said, and her cheeks pinkened. "I know."

"Unfortunately, my sister did not know until after they were married."

Flora looked down. "That must have been painful."

"Presumably," Wolfe mused.

Flora tilted her head. "You don't know?"

"She expressed anger."

"Tears?"

"I wouldn't tell you that."

"Of course. Forgive me."

He sighed. "Actually... There weren't any tears. She knew him only as a childhood friend who seemed terribly inefficient in setting a date." He shrugged. "Marriages have been built on much less."

"They've also been built on much more."

"Well. She can have her pick of people at the ball."

Flora smiled.

"Why does that amuse you?"

"Lady Isla has been to balls before. And from everything I've heard, she has no problem shining at them."

"She is a good McIntyre."

Flora continued to scrutinize him.

"What are you thinking?" Wolfe asked, even though he was not certain he wanted to know.

"I think you want to have her here. I think it's not about getting to marry her off at all."

"Nonsense." He shook his head rapidly.

The footman took away their plates. They'd finished dinner.

It was time for Wolfe to excuse himself, but he found himself lingering. "May I see the ballroom?"

"Naturally," she said. "I've been adding garlands to it."

They left the dining room, and he followed Flora through the corridors toward the ballroom. She moved gracefully, and her form was delicate and shapely.

Flora opened the heavy wooden door to the ballroom.

"It's wonderful," Wolfe murmured.

He'd always intended to compliment her, knowing she'd been working hard on it, but it truly was magnificent. The once plain room was transformed. Perhaps the fireplace did not have any carvings in its stone, and perhaps the walls were not paneled with elaborate wood designs, but it didn't matter. Mistletoe, holly and ivy hung from the ceiling.

He inhaled the scent of cloves and cinnamon, oranges and all manner of greenery.

"It's spectacular," he murmured.

"I'm glad," she said. "Some people consider it bad luck to hang greenery before Christmas, but I was hardly going to have the servants do it right on Christmas."

She was so beautiful. Golden light from the candles flickered over her skin. It danced in her hair and over her cheeks, and he wanted to touch it. He wanted to touch *her*.

"I think I have sufficient luck." He hesitated and then moved closer.

FLORA WAS DISTRACTED by his presence. His lips were so near hers.

"After all," the earl said, pulling her closer. "I've met you."

"You don't mean that," she said.

"I do," he said, more seriously.

His eyes locked hers, and everything changed. The world shifted.

The earl wasn't supposed to be staring at her like that. His eyes weren't supposed to be softening, and he wasn't supposed to be closing the distance between them.

"I must be the luckiest man in Scotland. The moment I needed assistance with this ball, you put up that advertisement." He pushed a wayward curl behind her ear causing her to flush. "I've never been one to celebrate Christmas, but I think I'm beginning to believe that Christmas may be magic." His eyes bore into hers.

This can't be happening, Flora thought as Wolfe leaned down, and she closed her eyes and lifted her chin to meet him.

He kissed her. The word was insufficient at describing the bliss that she experienced. She'd heard people praise the action of kissing, but she'd never known mere lips could make energy thrum through one's being.

Their lips danced, even though Flora had never realized dancing was a function lips could have. Wolfe's lips seemed to be the absolute master at it though, and she could feel his hands on her neck.

Finally, Wolfe pulled back, and Flora released him immediately, feeling a hollowness as he stepped away.

"Forgive me." Lord McIntyre broke away. "That was uncalled for."

She stared at him. Her heart beat madly.

"I should go." The earl moved, and his footsteps sounded heavy on the wooden floor. The noise reverberated in the room, a testament to its emptiness.

*****

DEVIL IT.

He shouldn't have kissed her.

And yet he'd almost kissed her before. Not kissing her seemed a difficult task.

He frowned. What sort of man couldn't keep their hands off a servant? *Not a good one.*

One wasn't supposed to desire one's maid. It was practically a cliché. One expected perhaps older, tottering aristocrats to occasionally succumb to mistiness when viewing their maids, but that could be attributed to the fact that tottering old men did not generally go out. Carriage rides were unpleasant even when one had one's full health. Wolfe was hardly tottering, and he'd been referenced frequently as one of London's top rogues.

Hiring Flora had seemed like a good idea, but he was wrong: it was the very worst one he'd ever had.

CHAPTER FOURTEEN

SHE'D BEEN KISSED.

Flora would have preferred if the man giving her first kiss had not looked horror stricken immediately afterward and she certainly would have preferred it if he had not rushed from the room.

Apart from those events, the kiss had been nice.

Exceedingly nice.

She stared at the mistletoe. Perhaps people said it was bad luck to refuse a kiss underneath it, but now she'd accepted a kiss, and nothing good had come from it.

She strode upstairs, removing the pins from her hair. She shouldn't have bothered trying to look pleasant. It hadn't taken the earl more than a few seconds to remember who she was, and why kissing her was a terrible matter. She wondered if he'd ever fled from any other woman he'd kissed. She suspected he had not.

She climbed into her bed. She'd thought it luxurious to have a single room when she arrived, but now she would be happy to have some company. Her heart continued to beat a nervous rhythm, not calmed by the frigid sheets.

She'd taken pride in her work as a maid. If she hadn't been good at her position, she never would have become the duchess's lady's maid. The earl had only complimented earlier on fulfilling her role as a Christmas consultant well, but accomplishment did not matter: in the end, she was simply a servant.

She supposed there must be some honor for him in the fact he didn't desire to take advantage of her, but she'd known him when she was a young girl. He was the only person who'd heard her music. And yet, he'd fled.

She attempted to sleep, and when she finally awoke, she was surprised that she'd managed any sleep at all. Last night's experience continued to course through her, and she dressed hastily, eager to concentrate on something, anything else.

Perhaps she could find the woodman after breakfast to ask him for help in cutting down a tree, and she marched down the stairs.

Mrs. Potter was already in the kitchen. "Good morning, dearie."

"Good morning."

Mrs. Potter's eyes glimmered. "The butler told me that you dined with the earl."

"Oh." Flora's heart tightened. "We did."

Mrs. Potter seemed to be always smiling, but Flora was certain her smile became even wider.

"Only to discuss Christmas matters," Flora said hastily. "It was quite dull."

"Mm...hmm." Mrs. Potter seemed to now be flicking meaningful glances at Flora.

"There are quite a lot of details," Flora continued.

Mrs. Potter rested a hand on her waist. "I've been working for the earl for years, and not a single time did he suggest that we dine together. And I assure you, there are quite a few details that he needs to be involved in as well."

Flora felt her skin warm.

"In fact," Mrs. Potter continued, "he's never even asked the butler to dine with him, though that may be because they're both men."

"It wasn't like that," Flora said.

"I think it was precisely like that," Mrs. Potter said, her tone more serious. "The earl is a good man, but you should be careful, dearie. He's not going to marry you."

"N-naturally not," Flora stammered.

She wanted to confide everything to Mrs. Potter, but after Christmas, Flora would leave for Cornwall, and Mrs. Potter would continue to work for the earl.

"Does the woodman still live in the cottage by the lake?" Flora asked.

"Yes, my dear," Mrs. Potter said.

"I wanted to call on him," Flora said. "I need his services to cut down a tree."

Mrs. Potter's eyes widened. "Is there a problem with one of the trees?"

"Oh, no, they're all magnificent," Flora said. "He evidently does a wonderful job maintaining the grounds."

"We all do what we can," Mrs. Potter said. "We don't have many visitors, but we do like the place to be nice."

Other manor homes had elaborate gardens attached to them, but that hadn't been Lord McIntyre's father's way. There were no mazes in which to be lost, and no rose bushes to smell, not that even the most fragrant flowers would be emitting any scent at this time of year.

"But I'm afraid Mr. Duncan is visiting his brother in Dundee. He's apparently taken sick, poor thing."

"Oh."

"That's nice that he was able to travel," she said.

"There's not that much work here," Mrs. Potter said, "what with the late earl and countess having passed on. Their children don't much care for this region. But it's good the new earl has kept all of us old staff on. We do appreciate it, even if we don't see him every year. It's not what other people would do. Some people just have their staff travel with them to save on expenses. No one would blame the earl if he decided to do that."

The earl was kind and thoughtful.

If the woodman was gone, she would have to cut down a tree herself. Flora put on her coat and boots after breakfast, and strode down toward the woodman's cottage. She'd done the same walk yesterday, and the countryside had seemed more beautiful than any other place. It remained lovely, but the wind seemed sharper than the day before. The earl's and her footsteps from the day before had been covered by new snow, and her feet seemed to sink deeper into the snow.

No matter.

Just reason why she had to get the tree today. Perhaps she could have asked a groom for assistance, but Flora wasn't wary of doing work. She could cut down a tree as well as any man. A groom or footman wouldn't have any more expertise than her.

There was a glimpse of the lake at the clearing, and she noticed a figure on it.

The earl.

The man was skating by himself, and her heart tightened. His movements were strong and athletic, and he easily glided from one side of the lake to the other. Her cheeks warmed at the memory of her grasping hold of his hand, fearful of venturing more than a few steps onto the ice. Perhaps he didn't flee because she was his servant. Perhaps he fled because she was much less accomplished than him.

She went to the woodman's cottage and unlocked the shed with the key the housekeeper had given her. She found the ax quickly, relocked the cottage and proceeded to the gathering of spruce trees. She grasped the ax in her hand. She'd never actually cut down a tree before, but the procedure seemed basic. She just had to hit the trunk with sufficient frequency and force until the tree toppled downward. The difficult thing would be to drag it back to the house, though she hoped the snow would at least lessen any damage. People might think the Christmas tree sufficiently strange without it appearing also misshapen.

She moved quickly, despite the temptation to watch the earl skate, until she came to the grove of spruce trees. Flora inhaled the pleasant scent and selected the most symmetrical tree. It was nearly twice her size.

A prickle of nervousness ran through her as she raised the ax. Her work before had not comprised of wielding medieval weapons, and she inhaled.

Then Flora struck the tree. The ax hadn't gone very far into the trunk, and yet it seemed to be stuck there. She bent down and yanked it out.

It's a start.

She bent down and proceeded to strike the same spot.

"What on earth are you doing?" A deep voice bellowed behind her, and she dropped the ax. It tumbled toward her toes, and then strong arms were about her and pulled her away. "You could have hurt yourself."

Flora's heart beat wildly, and she turned in the man's arms and tilted her head up.

Not that she had to look.

She already knew the owner of the voice.

It was the earl.

The man still clasped her in his arms. His eyes flashed, and she was conscious of the feel of his muscular arms as they held her tight. Her bosom was crushed against his chest.

"Let me go," she said. "Now."

WOLFE DROPPED HIS ARMS, and Flora stepped from them. He shouldn't have been holding her so tightly. He shouldn't have been holding her at all. "Forgive me."

He wobbled, and she looked down.

"You're wearing skates! You could have hurt yourself."

"I could have hurt myself? I'm not the person wielding a dangerous weapon."

"Those are more dangerous to your ankles," she said.

"I don't care about my ankles," he said. "I care about your life!"

She blinked. "It's simply an ax."

"And you're cutting down a tree! It could fall down and crush you."

"I would step away before it did that," she said. "Now I am working," she said. "You can kindly go."

"You mean... You don't intend to stop?"

"I'm cutting down a Christmas tree," she said. "I'm almost finished."

He gazed at the trunk of the tree. It did appear somewhat mangled.

"That's not a suitable task for you," he grumbled.

"And what is? Waking up at dawn for years? Scrubbing stairs? Until I became a lady's maid and stayed up late at night to worry about my mistress's attire? Truly, this task is not so unpleasant."

He felt his cheeks heat. Hades' Lair did not demand such physical labor from him.

"Forgive me," he said again.

"Just...go," she said, picking up the ax.

"Naturally." His voice sounded husky, and he shifted his legs awkwardly. He'd practically sprinted the few feet from the ice when he'd seen her, and he wasn't entirely certain how he'd managed to do so.

"You can hold onto my arm," she said.

"That's—er—unnecessary," he said.

"Last night you kissed me," she said brusquely. "And now you cannot even touch my arm?"

"I took advantage of the situation," he said. "Of your...beauty. I am deeply, deeply sorry. And I will not do so again."

"You think I'm beautiful?" she asked.

"That is not the part of the apology that you should be noting," he said.

"No?" Her eyes glimmered. *Devil it.* They looked like little stars. It was the sort of thing that made him want to give her more compliments, especially since they would all be utterly true.

"If you think I'm beautiful, why did you run?"

"Because I'm your employer, devil it. It wouldn't be suitable."

"You run a gaming hell," she said. "You're hardly a man with flawless morals."

"Well, I won't have any flaws that include hurting you," he said. "You're far too important."

"Is that so?"

"Obviously."

"Then why did you not ask me what I might desire?" she asked.

"What you desired?"

She nodded.

He didn't have an answer. "But surely you couldn't have wanted...?"

Her cheeks pinkened, and she looked away. "Please go."

Right.

He stumbled away, grasping hold of a tree branch, and then another one.

"Don't—"

Flora's call came too late. In the next moment, the branch, and Wolfe, toppled down. He was aware he was lying on spruce branches, that provided a bumpy barrier against the cold snow.

"Fiddle-faddle." Flora's voice sailed toward him, and in the next moment she was kneeling beside him. "How are you?"

"Still breathing," he said, but his voice was hoarse, and when Flora's head appeared beside him, her expression seemed distinctly worried.

"I'm so sorry, my lord," she said. "I didn't mean for you to—"

THE EARL'S CHRISTMAS CONSULTANT 111

"Fall?"

She nodded, and the pained expression remained on her face.

"It just means that I was right to be suspicious of you chopping down the tree," he said. "I recognized it as a danger...for me."

She gave him a wobbly smile. "Is there something I can do?"

"You can fetch my boots," he said, gesturing in their direction. "And then we can bring this tree to the manor house. At least it's fallen down."

"So you'll be able to walk?"

He rolled off of the spruce and flexed his feet experimentally. "I think so. I just have one question."

"Mm...hmm?"

He started to speak, but his heart seemed to have caught in his throat. He inhaled. "You told me that I didn't ask you what *you* desired."

"Oh." Her cheeks were certainly pinkening again, and she busied herself with smoothing the crushed spruce branches.

"What did you mean?"

She was silent, and for a horrible moment Wolfe thought he might have been imagining everything.

"I've known you since I was very young," she said, her tone more serious. "And I happen to be your servant now, but I don't want you to think of me as only that. Because I don't think of *you* simply as my employer."

"Then the kiss was not unwelcome?"

"It was not," she said.

The three words were simple, but for him, they seemed the most marvelous words in the world.

He squeezed her hand, and even though her hand was gloved, and even though his hand was gloved, energy still surged through him.

"I know you're a rogue," she said hastily. "And I know that I should stay far away from you. After all, you have a bad reputation," she said.

"Perhaps," he said lightly.

Wolfe had found the fact he ran a gaming hell often made people assume all manner of things about him. It didn't make him cruel, and unlike the people who visited the gaming hell, he was always working.

Wolfe knew that telling women that he was not truly as roguish and rakish as everyone said he was would be considered odd. He could let them believe that he spent his evenings wandering from ball to ball, bedding this woman and that woman, when truly the only place he was tethered was to the office in Hades' Lair.

"I've never harmed any woman," he said. "I think if you're an earl of a certain age you automatically get termed a rogue, whether you subscribe to their principles of seduction and abandonment or not. I *don't*."

She shot him a smile that seemed to twist his very insides. "You did leave the ballroom quite hastily last night."

He nodded.

"Besides," she said, more seriously. "I am leaving for Cornwall directly after Christmas. I won't see you again after that. I don't want to spend the rest of my time here avoiding you, or having you avoid me."

Cornwall.

It had seemed like a relief when she'd said for the first time that she didn't plan to stay in Scotland, or even London. And yet now the word caused his heart to pang, even though everyone knew Cornwall was supposed to make one think of chalky cliffs and quaint fishing villages.

"You're right," he said. "Then in that case..." He still lay on the snow, and he pulled her toward him. This time, he didn't hesitate. He wanted to kiss her. He wanted to taste her, to feel her lips dance with his.

The next minutes were pure bliss. It certainly didn't matter that he was being pressed deeper into the snow. All that mattered was that Flora was in his arms, and that she seemed to be just as happy to be there as he was. He'd been a fool before.

CHAPTER FIFTEEN

WOLFE ENTERED THE BALLROOM. The day had been blissful, even if it had involved dragging a bulky tree from the lake to the manor home, and even though Wolfe wasn't completely convinced having a tree in a ballroom was a good idea.

Flora had managed to wrangle the tree into a makeshift holder that involved a surprising amount of ingenuity. The tree had water, as if it were a rose or tulip sitting in a vase.

In five days Wolfe's sister would arrive, and in seven days it would be Christmas, and the ball would happen. Wolfe didn't want to think about what would happen on the eighth day. That was when his driver would take Flora to the village, and where she would take the first of many mail coaches that would take her all the way to Cornwall, and away from him forever.

Soon she would be gone, and the other servants might send him alternatively sympathetic looks or ones of disdain. He didn't want to break the trust that they had in him. And yet, if being properly involved meant not spending time with Flora, he couldn't do that. Flora's mere presence filled him with an energy he hadn't known he lacked. If Flora didn't mind his company, he would not retreat from her. He'd done that last night, and it had only caused his chest to ache and to have a sleepless night.

"I think we are going to have a late night decorating this tree."

She smiled, and the world was wonderful. His heart felt light, and he helped her attach thin candles onto the tree.

AFTER THEY'D EATEN, Flora contemplated the long stretch of ballroom. A single candle flickered golden light through the room, and her heart felt full.

"You look beautiful," Wolfe said.

"I didn't dress for dinner."

"You're already spectacular." He seemed to contemplate her and then he rose and strode toward her.

Most likely he was going to take her into his arms again, a new habit that Flora was already exceedingly fond of. Instead though he lowered himself into a bow.

"May I have this dance?" Wolfe asked.

Flora's eyes widened. "I don't know how to dance."

"Then I'll teach you," Wolfe said.

She nodded.

He stepped closer to her. "Personally I am quite fond of the waltz."

"It's Austrian," she said.

"I'm quite fond of things from that region of the world," Wolfe said airily, and he arranged her arms. "Now follow my lead."

He explained some of the intricacies of the dance, and then they danced together, even though there was no music, no guests and no ball.

"I think it must be very late," she said finally.

"And yet I'm not sleepy," he said.

"I'm not either," she confessed. Sleep was rather an impossible concept when one's heart seemed to leap and twirl.

Flora and Wolfe strode together through the corridor to their rooms. At the top of the first flight of stairs Wolfe tilted his head. "Would you like to see my room?"

The question was perhaps not one of only an option to evaluate interior décor.

Flora wasn't ready for the night to be over, and she nodded.

"Come." Wolfe took her hand and led her to his room.

He lit a candle and placed it on a bookcase.

"So this is what an earl's room looks like," Flora said.

"Does it remind you of a duchess's room?"

Flora assessed her surroundings. The room was a deep dark green, a testament to the man's love for nature. A large four poster bed sat in the room, facing large windows.

The sun had long set, and she only saw an inky black sky.

"This must be beautiful in the morning," she said.

She blushed. Perhaps it was somewhat inappropriate to mention what it might look like during the day. He was taller than her, and made her feel small. He was all muscular planes.

Desire pulsed through her body, soaring with a speed not even the most adept pianist could equal.

He pulled her closer to him, wrapping sturdy arms about her. The man wasn't supposed to feel so warm. It was winter. And yet touching him seemed to send flames dancing through her very soul.

And then his lips brushed against hers again. This time they were behind the sturdy wood door, most likely placed there centuries ago, and in no risk of collapsing.

THE EARL'S CHRISTMAS CONSULTANT 117

"It's wrong," he said finally.

"I don't care."

"You should leave," he said, but his voice sounded faint, and he still stroked her back. "I cannot harm your reputation."

"Though that is kind of you, I don't have much of a reputation to ruin."

"Indeed." He stopped stroking her momentarily, and his eyebrows rose up in obvious surprise.

"I mean because I'm going to Cornwall in a week," she said.

This time he stopped stroking her. "I'd prefer it if that was not the reason," he said. "I'm going to miss you."

"Oh?" She assessed him. Somehow she hadn't imagined him missing her. She'd known she would miss him...but that was different. His life was full and complete. She didn't even know if there was a piano in Cornwall, or if there was, whether she would be permitted to play.

"But you're still here now," Wolfe said, even though his voice wobbled somewhat.

He carried her in his arms and sat her down on the bed. Her heart thumped madly, and she was conscious of the momentousness of this moment.

His hands stroked her body, as if seeking to memorize each curve, as if finding the shape of each limb fascinating.

He traced her collarbone, and then he feathered kisses over it. Heat soared through her at his touch.

He clasped her toward him. "You are magnificent, my dear," he said firmly. "Utterly magnificent."

She wrapped her arms about him, and he drew her even closer.

"And now you must really go, before I ravish you," he said.

"I've heard that ravishing can be a nice experience," she said.

He groaned. "Flora."

Somehow the sound of her name on his lips was wonderful. She was still on the bed, and he kissed her more.

She'd been aware of his powerful presence long ago, and he'd reminded her of his athleticism when he'd skated so easily. But even though she may have said before that muscles could be intimidating, she only felt safe in his arms.

CHAPTER SIXTEEN

FLORA STIRRED IN A strange new bed that was more comfortable than anything she'd experienced.

"Good morning, my dear," Wolfe said, giving a kiss on her forehead.

She scrambled up. "I shouldn't be here."

"I disagree," he said lightly.

She glanced at the fire. It was lit, and it most certainly had not been lit late last night when they'd entered the room.

"I'm afraid the maid already noticed you," he said.

"So the secret is out," she said.

He nodded. "Do you mind?"

Her throat felt dry. "I suppose it doesn't matter," she said finally. "Since I'll go to Cornwall next week."

The happy expression on Wolfe's face vanished for a moment, but then he smiled. "I'm glad that you are not upset. Now let's have a leisurely morning."

"I'm not sure I know how to have a leisurely morning," she confirmed.

"Then it is good I am an expert in the matter," Wolfe said, kissing her again.

One kiss easily turned into multiple kisses.

It was no longer dark, and she could not pretend to herself that she was truly having a dream. This was Wolfe, and he was beside her, and it was wonderful.

He pulled her toward him, and she continued to kiss him, feeling a hunger she'd not known she'd possessed.

"WHAT WOULD YOU HAVE done if your father hadn't died?" Wolfe asked, stroking her hair absentmindedly.

"I always wanted to be a pianist," Flora mused.

"But I can help you with that," he said. "I know the music scene in London. There are many excellent charitable organizations that can be of use to you, some of which I am on the board for. Once I return to London I can do that. You needn't go to Cornwall at all."

Somehow the thought of her being in London filled him with joy.

"No, that's not possible."

"You mean, you desire to go to Cornwall?"

Cornwall was far away. If she went there, they wouldn't see each other again.

His heart heavied. He was offering her a chance to do what she loved most in the world, yet she would rather be a companion to a woman she'd never even met before.

The only logical reason for her action was that she didn't want to be around him. Perhaps he'd been mistaken about everything. Perhaps she didn't want to be here in his bed after all.

"I'm sorry we spent the night together. I thought you desired it. But I understand you might feel, because of your position...."

"No, no, no," she said quickly. "You don't understand."

He blinked.

Not understanding at all was not the most flattering manner in which to describe his powers of perception.

She touched his hand. "There's something I haven't told you. Something important."

"You can tell me," he said gently.

"I don't like to speak of it," she said, "and I haven't told anyone else about this. As you know, I became a maid ever since my father died." She looked straight ahead, willing herself not to remember certain things. "He wasn't sick when he died and he didn't have an accident. He was murdered."

"Murdered?"

"Stabbed multiple times. There was blood." She looked away.

"I'm so sorry," he said. "Did they ever catch the man?"

She turned toward him. "I saw it happen and I never told anyone."

"Flora." Evidently he had it all wrong. "But I don't understand. Why didn't you say anything? I'm sure the magistrate would have been grateful for any information you had."

"Oh, they don't even know he was killed," Flora said. "They simply think he vanished. I'm sure the person who killed him had paid some people to put his body in the Thames." She shrugged. "Perhaps he's buried in the backyard for all I know. It's not important. He's dead."

"Oh."

It must have happened when Wolfe was fighting overseas, before he started Hades' Lair, and before he became involved in London's music community.

He'd inquired once about him from someone. One of his friends had mentioned he'd been in London for a while and had returned to Europe.

"I'm so sorry," he said. "So you were a witness to a murder."

"And the person saw me," Flora said, staring in front of her again. "That's why I had to disappear. I couldn't be found. Because if the person saw me again, they would want to make certain I remained silent."

"What a horrible thought," he said.

She gave a wobbly smile.

"You've been so brave," he continued.

"One does what one has to do."

"So the reason you're going to Cornwall is because of its remoteness."

"Yes. I'll be a companion to an older widow. You know how difficult it is to go from London to Cornwall."

"Indeed." It was a days-long journey. A week if one wanted any comfort. The roads were muddy and difficult to pass through, much like visiting Scotland itself.

"Do you know why he was murdered?" Wolfe asked.

Flora shook her head. "No, I don't know. My father was a good and kind man."

"I know," Wolfe said, and he squeezed her hand.

She smiled softly at him, and his heart thundered. He couldn't imagine that such a nice man had been killed.

"Well, you know who did it, so I will take you back to London, contact the magistrate, and ensure that the person is behind bars and can never hurt you again."

Flora's smile wobbled. "The man in question is very powerful, and I'm certain his word is more important than mine, especially since no body was ever found."

She took his hand in hers. "Right now your family members haven't arrived yet. They won't arrive until the day before Christmas, and—"

"We have these days for ourselves," Wolfe said.

And he kissed her.

Again. And again. And again.

CHAPTER SEVENTEEN

FLORA HAD BEEN SLEEPING in his room every single night. It would all end at Christmas, but now it seemed unfathomable for her not to join him.

The door opened, and Wolfe opened his eyes. Sarah must be coming to light the fireplace. He glanced at Flora. All he wanted to do was to pull her closer to him and to cover her in dozens of kisses. He wanted to claim her lips again and again with his own.

"Wolfe?"

Maids generally did not address him by his first name. Maids generally did not address him with anything except "My Lord," usually accompanied by a blush. This voice was strong, confident and definitely female.

Isla?

"You have company?" Isla asked.

Flora stirred beside him, and Wolfe jumped from his bed.

"What are you doing here?" he asked.

"I live here," his sister said, assessing him. Her gaze remained fixed on the bed. "You seem to have acquired many blankets."

"It was quite cold in the night," Wolfe said.

Isla shuddered. "I know. I traveled here in it. I thought you would be grateful I didn't wake you then."

THE EARL'S CHRISTMAS CONSULTANT 125

"Er—yes." Wolfe felt the back of his neck prickle, even though it was distinctly cold in the room.

Isla had to leave.

"I didn't expect to see you," he said, forcing a smile on his face.

She raised her eyebrows. "You all but begged me to come. Tell me about this Christmas ball."

"Ah, yes." He smiled, contemplating all the merriment Flora had already brought on the manor and village.

Isla narrowed her eyes. "You're acting strangely."

"Christmas spirit, my dear," he said nonchalantly.

Her eyes remained narrow, and her gaze was on the bed. "You haven't got anyone?"

Wolfe tried to not look at Flora, relieved she hadn't woken up. He adjusted the blanket, ascertaining neither her splendid luscious locks nor her sumptuous form were in view.

Perhaps he did manage to avoid glancing at her, but something in his expression must have changed, for Isla's eyes widened.

"Who's that?"

"What?"

"Th-that lump—" Isla pointed and Wolfe hurried from the bed and led Isla into the adjoining room.

Flora was already stirring. He suspected she did not want to be met with his sister's irritation. Heavens, he didn't want it, and he'd had decades of practice.

"Then it is a woman," Isla said triumphantly.

"N-nonsense," Wolfe said, conscious he didn't desire to damage Flora's reputation.

"Then why on earth are we standing here?"

"Er—" Wolfe swallowed hard. His throat felt dry.

"You lecture me about responsibility, and then you drag some poor woman off to this manor house—"

"There was no dragging involved," Wolfe said, outraged.

"I hope you didn't help yourself to the servants," Isla said. "That's the sort of thing only disreputable men do. Which obviously you are, though somehow I never took you for a man who—"

Warmth invaded Wolfe's cheeks. This was the sort of conversation one wasn't supposed to have with one's sister, no matter how cultured and well-traveled she was.

The worst thing was...she was correct. Flora *was* a servant. It didn't seem that way. She didn't wear a uniform and her job differed from that of a maid. They'd even known each other as children. She'd even dined in the nursery with him and the other children of the manor house. It seemed strange to think of her as solely a servant.

He hadn't met a woman of the *ton* who could play so well, who was so intelligent. Flora had taken this position for her safety.

And yet—

Flora was hardly a woman of the *ton*. He would never chance upon her at a ball, even with the most unfashionable wallflowers and bluestockings. No matchmaking mama or proud papa would ever thrust her in his direction. Flora's own parents were dead, but even if they had been alive, their class would not have equaled that of earl, even if they were far more talented and kind than his own father had ever been.

"You're an impossible man," Isla huffed. "Are you going to tell me?"

"Naturally not," Wolfe said, and for a very brief moment hurt seemed to descend upon his sister's face. It was only for a moment though, and then her features steeled and she was once again the impenetrable ice aristocrat.

"DID YOU NEED TO HAVE somebody in your bed, Wolfe?" A woman's voice sailed through the air, and Flora stiffened.

She was not in her normal bed.

She was in...the earl's.

Memories of last night and everything wonderful, everything precious, inundated her mind, and for a moment everything was perfect.

She turned to the other side of the bed. Wolfe had been there throughout the night, giving a gentle snore entirely at odds with his roguish image, one that had made her smile. He'd emanated warmth, even after the brick in the bed had cooled.

Now though he was absent.

The bed might possess ample numbers of blankets, but they couldn't disguise his muscular form.

He was gone.

Flora blinked and rubbed the sand from her eyes.

She recognized the amaretto timber of his voice, but it was joined by an alto voice that she could not place. She listed the maids whom he might be speaking to, but none of them sounded so refined, and none of them tended to enter into long conversations with him.

Another woman?

Flora pushed away the flicker of jealousy. Wolfe was well-regarded with women. Even she knew that, and she'd been a maid in a different house.

Besides, she could hardly have any claim to him. She'd entered into bed for no other reason than that she adored him, even though that was the same reason that had felled other women who'd adored other men.

Perhaps there was another world in which her father had not been murdered, and in which she could have married the second son of an aristocrat and no one would have minded. But that had changed once she'd taken on the position of maid for the Butterworths, and the added responsibility of arranging Christmas for the earl did not change her low position.

Flora wrapped the sheet around her, conscious of her state of undress. The sheets were too soft, the bed too luxurious, for her.

No one could find her here.

Wolfe wouldn't want that, and she wanted Wolfe to be happy.

Clothes.

She needed clothes.

She swung her gaze around the room, spotting her chemise, dress and stockings dangling in various corners, as if to emphasize the utter inappropriateness of last night.

The adjoining door opened, and Lady Isla stepped inside.

Flora wrapped the sheet around her quickly, conscious that the action was unlikely to mask her unclothed state completely. Her shoulders were bare, and her hair tousled in a manner utterly not in keeping with anyone with a modicum of decency.

THE EARL'S CHRISTMAS CONSULTANT 129

Lady Isla narrowed her eyes. The woman was splendid, despite the early hour. Her coiffure emanated exquisiteness.

Lady Isla hesitated. "You seem familiar."

Flora bit her lip.

There'd been a time when Isla had played with Flora. She'd been older and perhaps prone to bossiness. She'd overwhelmed Flora with a list of her dolls and their accompanying vast collection of clothes. And yet, they'd enjoyed themselves.

"Is that—?" Lady Isla's confident voice wobbled, and Flora's chest tightened.

"Greta," Lady Isla said softly. She swung her gaze to Wolfe. "What is *she* doing here?"

"You recognized her?" Wolfe's voice croaked.

"Naturally," Lady Isla said. "Now can we please speak in private?"

Wolfe shot an apologetic look to Flora, and Isla opened the door to the adjoining room.

"I'm not alone," Isla said.

"Whom did you bring? Admiral Fitzroy and his wife?"

"You needn't appear so scandalized. They are very pleasant. No, I didn't bring them. They are in Southern France. The Duke and Duchess of Vernon are here along with Lord and Lady Hamish Montgomery."

"Indeed?" Wolfe found himself giving a pleased smile.

"And everyone will be scandalized of your treatment of the duchess's former maid."

"I'm treating her well."

"I don't think I need tell you they might think it in bad taste to discover you've been bedding the duchess's former lady's maid. Rather vulgar."

"There was nothing vulgar about it," he said defiantly.

Isla raised her eyebrows. "I hardly think you would like me to invite my groomsman up to spend the night with me."

"Naturally not. That's—er—quite different. Quite different indeed."

Isla narrowed her eyes. "Is it?"

The question rushed through his mind.

"I heard our names," a cheerful voice said, and the duke peered through the open door.

"Callum!" Wolfe said, mustering enthusiasm. "How delightful to see you."

"I wouldn't miss it," the duke said merrily.

HIS FRIENDS WERE HERE. Flora heard the voices. Christmas was truly beginning now.

Even though it had always been her favorite time of year, it occurred to her she would not be able to spend more time alone with Wolfe. He would be busy hosting his friends, and he would not want to deign to admit he'd spent more time than was appropriate with her.

She swallowed hard. She dressed hastily, wishing she'd worn a dress without quite so many buttons. She then smoothed her hair in the silver framed mirror in Wolfe's room. Her heart beat, and she tried to create some semblance of respectability.

No one could ever know.

She opened the door a crack. She didn't hear anyone in the hallway. They all seemed to be convened in the room beside.

THE EARL'S CHRISTMAS CONSULTANT 131

Finally, she swallowed hard and proceeded to march down the corridor.

She made it only ten paces before she heard a voice.

"Flora, my dear!"

Normally Flora enjoyed her past mistress's sister's company, but now she halted suddenly, as if she'd been turned to stone.

"I can't believe it! It's you!" Lady Hamish Montgomery continued. "Hamish! Look who I found in the corridor!"

In the next moment Lord Hamish Montgomery, the Duke of Vernon, and the Duchess of Vernon had surrounded her in the corridor. She watched as Lady Isla and finally Wolfe joined. She didn't meet Wolfe's eyes.

Flora's heart beat madly. She'd just exited the earl's room. In the morning. Anyone would find it odd that she was upstairs.

And they didn't even know she was here. She averted her eyes as if she could in any way hide from Lady Hamish Montgomery. It was impossible.

"I'm working here for the earl," she said.

"McIntyre, you need a lady's maid?" The duke slapped Wolfe on the back, and Lord Hamish Montgomery joined him in laughter.

"The solution to having slightly long hair is to cut it off, not to hire a lady's maid," the duke continued.

They seemed so happy. She looked at them but she saw no disapproval in their expressions. Only slight confusion.

They don't know. They don't suspect.

She'd just been leaving his quarters, but they always saw her as a servant. They didn't see anything untoward about her appearance, only the fact that she was in Scotland at all.

"I mean..." The duchess looked at her. "You said you were going far away, but I didn't expect to find you precisely here. Otherwise you could have come with us, couldn't you have?"

"Naturally," the duke said. "My wife already misses you as lady's maid. Others are just not as good."

"I can certainly believe that," Wolfe said. "But she is not just a lady's maid."

The others rolled their eyes.

"Well, you do not require a lady's maid," Lord Hamish Montgomery said.

"Flora is our Christmas consultant," Wolfe said.

"There's such a thing?" The duke narrowed his eyes.

"There's all manner of interesting and new positions," the duke's brother said, evidently eager to contradict his twin.

"She is responsible that the festivities for the holiday season go well."

"Oh, that does sound most fascinating," the duchess said kindly. "And you're doing something quite apart from hair and mending."

The duchess's sister gave her a curious look.

"She is exceptional," Wolfe said again, as if worried that the duchess might think her only suited to clothes.

"How extraordinary. Not that I would doubt it," the duchess's sister said. "You always were a very sweet maid."

"It's quite far to take her," the duke mused.

"It is a most important position. And I assure you, you will have a most delightful time here," Wolfe declared, shifting the conversation away from her. "I am so happy you could attend. Perhaps we can go down to the breakfast room together. I'm famished."

"What a magnificent idea," Lady Isla said. "We can leave your Christmas consultant in peace to continue her work."

The others followed her down the stairs.

The duchess turned. "I'm really so excited to see you here. We must talk at some point."

"That would be lovely." Flora smiled, but her heart ached.

It didn't matter. She had work to do. She tried to move briskly and she tried not to have her mind linger on Wolfe.

Flora continued down the corridor, opened the door to the servant's staircase and then descended down to the kitchen. She would eat something too.

The housekeeper and maid looked at her with pity. They knew what had happened, and they knew now what her new state was.

"I'm sorry, love," Mrs. Potter said, giving her a drink. "You shouldn't get too close to the master."

She raised her chin. "I'm quite well, Mrs. Hopkins. I have some work to do."

"The ballroom looks beautiful," one of the maids said.

She smiled. "I think I'll make some snowflakes to join them. Is there paper?"

The housekeeper nodded. "I have some in the pantry. How many do you need?"

"As many as I can have for you to have sufficient paper until you can order more."

"Then you must be quite fond of snowflakes." The housekeeper smiled.

"I am." She formed snowflakes with the paper, remembering going skating with Wolfe and how actual real life snowflakes had fallen over them and had led them to the cottage and had led them to so much more. It was a good memory, the very best memory she could have.

Then she could go to Cornwall and then she could say that for a few days at least she'd lived in bliss. Perhaps not everyone could say that.

CHAPTER EIGHTEEN

WOLFE HAD SEEN FLORA leave dozens of times before. But this time was different. This time it meant everything had changed.

"Your visitors arrived last night," Hamish said. "Lord Pierce and Mr. Warne."

"Good, I'm glad," Wolfe said. "Have they been good guests so far?"

"I think they're still traumatized from the carriage journey. Not that they would admit it."

Wolfe chuckled.

"They mentioned going into town tomorrow though. I thought I wouldn't drag them here for breakfast."

"Ah. I'm glad. I want the ball to be when they first see McIntyre Manor."

"When it is at its very finest?" Hamish asked. "Callum mentioned you are trying to matchmake Isla. You're a good brother."

"I try to be. I thought I would give her some options."

"Are you certain she desires to marry?"

Wolfe laughed. Of course Isla wanted to marry. That was obvious. What woman didn't want to marry? The whole season was filled with women utterly desiring of marrying. He knew.

He saw how desirous they were to dance with him, despite his reputation.

"You've grown quite amusing since you married," Wolfe said.

"I wasn't trying to make a joke," Hamish grumbled.

"Ah, there's that serious nature again. I think I'll be spending more time here," Wolfe confessed.

"Truly?" Hamish's eyebrows rose. "When you have Hades' Lair? I thought that was going well."

"It is going well," Wolfe said. "That doesn't mean I desire to stay there."

Hamish gave him a strange look.

"What is it?"

"This region is isolated. Are you certain you would be happy?"

"I would be," Wolfe said.

"Hmph."

"I suppose it's an age thing," Hamish mused. "What you require, Lord McIntyre, is a wife. Were you aware that Lord Pierce is in possession of a sister?"

"I was not."

"Well, he is in fact," Hamish said. "Apparently she's debuting this season. You can snatch her up in January."

Wolfe shifted his legs over the floor. "I have no desire to be saddled with some eighteen year old bride."

"Come now. Lord Pierce's sister has been schooled in the finest finishing schools. She will make a most excellent countess. I'm not simply saying that because Lord Pierce lets me win when we play whist together."

"I don't know," Wolfe said.

"Apparently she is in possession of Lord Pierce's blond hair, and I remember you remarking at one point that you were partial to the fairer strands of the hair spectrum.

"I've changed my mind. I prefer brown hair."

"Well, as someone with brown hair, I am glad your tastes have matured, though I imagine Lord Pierce's sister has other fine attributes not relating to her hair color as well. On the other hand, there are bound to be other debutantes who meet your new hair preferences more completely."

"I don't want to meet anyone in the season," Wolfe confessed.

"Suit yourself. But you might be happier with someone. I certainly am."

"I agree," Wolfe said. "I don't believe Miss Pierce is the woman for me."

"Her father is an earl, so she is Lady Isabella."

"Lady Isabella then. I don't believe Lady Isabella is the woman for me."

"Well. Isla has been spending time with Admiral Fitzroy's wife, which reminds me that Admiral Fitzroy has a niece. Lady Theodosia. I think she might be suitable. She is a bit silly, but she does like poetry, which must show some sign of intelligence."

"One would hope so," Wolfe said. "The thing is I may have already met the right person."

"Indeed?" There was an odd glimmer in Hamish's eyes. "That's good. That's the hardest part."

Wolfe tried to smile, but he couldn't. Perhaps normally meeting someone was the most important part, but this was different. He was an earl. Didn't he have some responsibilities? He couldn't really just run off with a former maid of all service.

He would be starting a married life with scandal. His children would be born into that same scandal. It was really not the McIntyre way. At all. The McIntyre way was all about sacrifice. He'd been told that many times. Sacrifice even when everything was difficult.

His father had been stern, and he hadn't been nice, and perhaps he'd been quite bad. Callum was convinced his father had acted truly malevolently against Callum's aunt, though at this point no evidence existed. Besides, he did know his father had acted with the interests of the family in mind. Could Wolfe ignore all that sacrifice? Love matches were things for villagers, for people who did not have to think about families, who did not have to think about how a match might affect business interests. And yet, with all his heart he adored her. The thought of all that logic couldn't sway him from the belief that the best thing for him, the best thing for her, would be to marry.

He sighed. "Can I speak to you in confidence?"

Hamish raised his eyebrows. "I thought you were closer with my brother."

"You have the reputation for being more sensible."

"That is true. It's because of my massive intelligence. Did I mention that I received a new commission?"

At any other time Wolfe would have rolled his eyes. "I'm not doing that badly either."

Hamish shrugged. "Perhaps. Now what is it."

"There's this woman. She's divine. Like the sun."

"Though I imagine her hair is more dark?"

"Yes."

"I gathered that," Hamish said lightly. "Comes with my massive intelligence."

"So there is this dark-haired woman who is utterly beguiling."

"Quite. Though it's not her appearance that draws me to her."

"I imagine that's part of it."

Wolfe nodded. "Yes, that's part of it. But none of this would have happened if it had just been her appearance."

He'd seen pretty maids before, but he'd never desired them. They'd blended into his space, like a nicely formed sconce or sideboard. Something he noticed on occasion, appreciated, but hardly dwelled on.

Devil it, he did dwell on Flora. She was everything.

"If she is so wonderful, what exactly is the issue with her?" Hamish asked.

"There's no issue with her."

"Well, then, why don't you grab your mother's ring from her jewelry collection, run after her, and propose?"

"Just like that?"

"Why not?" Hamish asked.

"What if we've only really known each other a few weeks?"

Hamish snorted. "That's more time than I'd known my wife. before we married. And trust me, we are exceedingly happy."

"You have changed."

"You don't need to meet someone over dozens of balls, have two dances with them each time, and then call on them in the presence of their mothers and any aunts to know whether one wants to marry them or not." Hamish tilted his head.

"Now tell me. Are we talking about your affection for your Christmas consultant?"

Wolfe swallowed hard. "How did you know?"

"She has dark hair and, though my heart is forever my wife's, I can see there is a certain symmetry in her face that you may deem appealing, but I've never seen two people make more effort at not looking at each other."

"Do you think anyone else noticed?"

"No. I only just put it together, and—"

"—you have a massive intelligence."

"Oh, now you're teasing me."

Wolfe smiled.

"Since she does work for you I would be more cautious. She should not feel compelled to accept any offer you might give her."

Wolfe swallowed hard. "Her last day is at the Christmas ball."

"Well. That makes it simple. You don't have long to wait. You can propose after the ball."

"Oh." Wolfe blinked. He'd thought Hamish would be more disapproving. The man had done his best to stop his brother's match, when he'd deemed him to be making an inappropriate marriage.

"Just so she knows she has the option to get into a carriage and leave. The position really ends after the Christmas ball?"

Wolfe nodded. "Yes. She has a position in Cornwall that begins in January."

"Then she can decide how ideal the position in Cornwall is. That's simply my advice."

"It's good advice," Wolfe said.

He resisted his urge to bound down the stairs and go after her, and say that spending his days with his friends did not surpass spending his time with her. Besides, this day had been about his sister Isla. He mustn't forget that. It would do no good causing a scandal beforehand, and Isla had made her opinions on Flora quite clear. Even though they'd been friends at one point, Isla did not approve of Flora in Wolfe's bed, and he hardly thought Isla would approve of Flora as his wife.

"Just a few more days."

"One thing you're wrong about is that I will not slide my mother's ring on her finger."

"No?"

"My parents' marriage is nothing I would like to replicate."

"Then perhaps the occasion calls for visiting a jeweler."

"Indeed. You mentioned that the others wanted to go into town? Why don't we all go together? That will give Flora time to work on everything."

"Splendid."

Wolfe and Hamish left the room to find the others. At least going to town would provide him of some distraction, and in the meantime he could ensure that the ball was everything Flora desired as well.

Perhaps Flora was working, but Wolfe had a new task, one only for himself. He wanted to create the most wonderful ball in the world, for her. He wanted her to have the very best time imaginable. He wanted her heart to soar, and he wanted her to feel special, because she was. She was more special than any of the guests he'd invited.

CHAPTER NINETEEN

ANY DELUSIONS FLORA might have had that Wolfe intended their liaison to be anything more vanished. Wolfe was always with his friends, and she was alone decorating the huge ballroom. She ironed ribbons that she'd purchased with Wolfe's help, trying not to become sentimental. He'd been more skeptical of glossy fabrics than she was, stating a preference for the durability of linen that was decidedly a masculine instinct as well as an enthusiasm for tweed and tartan fabrics that suited his Scottish countryside upbringing. *No matter.* There was no point in growing sentimental at the sight of the ribbons. At least she knew now this was the end. She tried to think about how that could be a good thing, even though it seemed like just a minute more in his company, ten minutes more, would be everything.

She sighed. Tomorrow would be the Christmas ball, and the next day she would leave for her perfect position in Cornwall to be a companion to a young widow in a far off location where Mr. Warne would no longer find her.

She tried to push away the joy she'd found in the manor and the friendly staff. The staff in Cornwall were probably friendly as well, and it was wrong of her to feel any doubt. In fact, it would be good to go and not wonder if every footstep she heard was Wolfe and whether he would come to her room.

He never had.

Once she left, she wouldn't have to studiously avoid looking at him when he was in her vision, lest she wonder when she looked at him why his face was rigid, devoid of any smile, devoid of anything else, that made her heart yearn.

She worked rapidly. She would make this ball wonderful, and that would be it. This would all be a memory, a foolish youthful indiscretion before she embarked on a road to certain spinsterhood.

THE SLEIGH SPED OVER the slopes, approaching the town's familiar gray buildings. Isla's coiffure was perhaps slightly less immaculate than when she entered the sleigh, though her smile was wide.

"How could I have forgotten this?" she asked. "It's delightful."

Wolfe grinned. "We'll have to make certain this becomes part of the new McIntyre family tradition."

"In addition to an elaborate ball?"

He nodded. "Naturally."

"I visited the ballroom," she said, her tone more serious. "It does look spectacular."

"Doesn't it?" He beamed, and his mind dwelled on Flora's talents.

Isla gave him an odd look.

The driver stopped in the center of the square, outside of the public house, and soon Hamish and Callum, their wives, and Mr. Warne and Lord Pierce arrived.

"Don't tell me they've brought their guests," Isla said, in a mournful tone that sounded suspiciously like a groan.

Perhaps Mr. Warne or Lord Pierce might become his sister's husband. Wolfe glanced at her, conscious of wanting to see what her impression of the men would be.

"You may find them amusing," he said.

His sister's eyes narrowed.

Devil it.

She was always clever.

"Both men are quite fine and unattached," he declared, despising the slight defensiveness in his voice.

"One wonders why they're unattached," she said.

"Perhaps it's because they haven't met you."

She laughed. "I've seen both of them in balls at London."

Well.

This was evidently not going to be a case of love at first sight. *No matter.* He hadn't loved Flora at once either, but he absolutely did now.

"I imagine you haven't spent time with them," Wolfe said.

"I never saw the need," Isla grumbled.

"Be nice to them."

"That's not my natural inclination," Isla said, and Wolfe rolled his eyes. "The men might think I desire to marry them."

"You mustn't speak like that," he said. "There's much to be commended about marriage."

"Indeed? According to the man who's never shown any interest in courting anyone before, despite the heavy suggestions of multiple matchmaking mamas and proud papas? And who's spending nights with one of his servants? Really, no sense of morals at all."

"No, I think it is important for you to have someone good in your life."

"How hypocritical," Isla murmured.

Wolfe winced. Perhaps it had been hypocritical when he'd arranged this, but he now knew it was true. His time with Flora had been wonderful, and he wanted Isla to experience the same. She couldn't simply flit from house party to house party indefinitely. That was no life, even if he had tarnished her reputation. He was determined to make it better.

"Just be nice to them," he said curtly, and soon he approached the others.

"Lord McIntyre. Lady Isla." Lord Pierce dipped down into a bow and kissed Isla's hand. Wolfe gave him an approving nod.

Lord Pierce was somewhat stocky and was active in parliament. Wolfe imagined Isla would find his parliament activity dull, though he hoped she would find his title respectable. Isla had of course always appreciated music. Both Lord Pierce and Mr. Warne frequented music gatherings.

He strode through the streets of the town.

"My lord." A few people nodded to him.

"I didn't realize you were so acquainted with the people here," Callum remarked.

"Perhaps I'm more memorable than you are."

Callum frowned. "Nonsense."

Wolfe had always assumed London to be far superior, and he dismissed this town as being close to where his parents had lived, but he was enjoying returning here, even if his last trip here, with Flora, had been decidedly more enjoyable.

He resisted the temptation to drag the others into the haberdashery. He doubted the experience would be the same without her.

The sun shone brightly, and the weather was colder than on the other days. The brisk wind constantly nipped at the back of his neck and the place where his gloves and coat sleeves met, as if trying to reach any way to chill him, no matter his carefully chosen woolen attire.

Callum's wife drew Callum's attention to something, and soon Wolfe found himself walking with Mr. Warne. Callum was not particularly close to Mr. Warne, but he often found the man at musical events.

"What a lovely town," Mr. Warne declared. "I am enjoying it."

"Good," Wolfe said.

"You don't mind the cold?" Isla's lips curled, and Wolfe shot her a warning glance.

"It is a welcome change from the south coast," Mr. Warne said.

"Where are you from?" Isla asked, and Wolfe sent her an approving nod.

She was making conversation. This was wonderful.

"I'm from Sussex," Mr. Warne said. "Near Hastings."

"Ah, a place abundant with smugglers," Callum murmured.

"Yes," Mr. Warne said. "Quite."

"I heard they can be quite violent in that area," Hamish's wife said.

"Perhaps that's why he's moved to London," Isla said, "and perhaps it's why he doesn't find it too cold here."

"It would be a long way for smugglers to come here," Wolfe demurred, "even if this is on the coast and even if this area does have a good relationship with France."

Mr. Warne gave a polite smile. "I find the landscape more dramatic. It suits my sensibilities."

"A romantic man," Wolfe said. "Quite Germanic."

"I've met some Germans in my time," Mr. Warne said.

"Do you enjoy their music?" Wolfe asked curiously.

"How could I not? Especially the newer things that are happening there. So romantic. So much emotion. Has there even been a better composer than Beethoven?" The man spoke with passion, and Isla's eyes practically glittered.

Wolfe stepped away so the two might continue their conversation. Isla shared his passion for music.

Wolfe was happy Isla seemed content. He entered into a conversation with Lord Pierce. The man's interest in music was decidedly less developed. Lord Pierce's interests were more in the direction of helping others, and he proceeded to speak about intricate politics instead.

Wolfe eventually made an excuse so that he could visit the jeweler. When he found the group, they were debating the merits of visiting The Lamb's Inn.

"Let's go to the tavern," Callum said. "I haven't been there in years."

"I'm sure it's not proper to take the ladies there," Hamish said.

"Ha," Callum scoffed. "This isn't London. We can find a private room there."

Wolfe followed them into the tavern. It didn't matter what they did now. He had the ring.

He entered the now familiar tavern, ducking slightly to avoid the low medieval beams. Wolfe scanned the crowd. Several of the men had been there when Flora and he had been there last.

"Ah, it's the earl," one of the people in the tavern said.

"Where's your lady friend?" one person asked.

The others looked at him.

"Lady friend?" Callum asked, and Wolfe attempted to appear unfazed by the comment. He'd promised himself to not reveal anything about Flora, and he certainly was not going to break that vow before Lord Pierce and Mr. Warne.

"They played the most beautiful piano together," one man said, and his eyes took on a dreamy tone.

"Is that so?" Mr. Warne asked.

"Aye. It's rare to see a woman play so well."

Wolfe cleared his throat. "They are referring to my Christmas consultant."

Mr. Warne's eyes widened. Evidently Harrison was not the only person who found Flora's occupation unexpected.

"You're not speaking about Flora?" Callum asked.

"I am," Wolfe said. "She is remarkably talented."

"Like an angel," the burly publican said, and his eyes glazed, as if he were even now remembering her music.

Wolfe didn't blame him in the slightest.

"How extraordinary," Callum said.

"Remarkable," his wife breathed.

"You appear shocked," Mr. Warne said, addressing Callum.

"She used to be my wife's maid," Callum said.

"A maid?" Mr. Warne's eyes narrowed, and he steepled his fingers together. "How very extraordinary to find her so talented. I would have thought it odd that she'd even know how to play."

"We weren't aware of it. But we would have let her practice had we known."

"Oh, indeed," the duchess said.

"We don't need to speak about her more," Wolfe said quickly. He knew she respected her privacy.

"Oh, but you must. She truly is such a good musician," the publican said.

She was.

All these people were so eager to have her play for them again. If he could not convince Flora to remain with him, he wanted to give her the opportunity to play her compositions before an audience. It was her dream after all. She'd never even heard her work be played before. The musicians he'd hired would be able to do that.

If she did decide to stay with Wolfe, she might still be nervous of playing in London, even under his protection.

But this was Scotland. This was the upper, fairer portions of Scotland, away from whatever harm she'd come from. Why not have her play here?

He smiled, contemplating how he might make the ball even nicer.

CHAPTER TWENTY

THE MUSICIANS WERE practicing, and the house was filled with Christmas music, even though their guests would not arrive for a few hours. Wolfe paced the ballroom, but everything was perfect. Garlands draped from wooden beams in the old ballroom, melding well with the old fashioned wood. His parents had always despised the room, thinking it should be more modern, more like the glittering ballrooms that let in lots of light, even though people only danced in them at dark. Those ballrooms had cerulean ceilings with gods and goddesses perched on clouds wearing very little. But there was something about this starkness that Wolfe appreciated. It was not pretentious, in fact with Flora's touch it felt like home, more even than when he was a child.

The air was infused with the scent of oranges and cloves. Fire danced in the great stone fireplace in one corner of the room. Flora had found dark red curtains that suited the Christmas spirit and had draped them over the windows, including the ones that led to the few balconies.

Flora flitted about the ballroom, making everything look lovely. It was difficult for him not to stare at her.

It would be easy to say she was below him, merely because of her birth. Many other people would say the same. Perhaps if he married her he would spend the rest of his life noting the raised eyes that lifted when they entered a room together.

Devil it.

He wanted to speak to her. He crossed the ballroom, despising the way her eyes widened, as if she didn't expect to see him.

"It's you," she breathed.

"You appear surprised," he said softly.

"We had a good time. That is all. You needn't be speaking more. You certainly haven't been doing that lately."

"Oh, Flora," he said. "I have longed to speak to you."

Her eyes knit with confusion. "To say goodbye?"

"No," he said.

For a moment her face seemed to crumple. "I am leaving in the morning."

"Look," he said. "Just promise to save me a waltz."

"But I'm a guest," she said.

"And yet I cannot think of a lovelier waltz partner," he said, taking her hands in his. He wanted to take her in his arms and he wished the ballroom were not filled with quite so many footmen.

He left her, wanting to say everything to her, but not wanting to disrupt his sister's event.

Finally, horses pranced outside the windows. The first guests were arriving. Festive jingles rang out, and Wolfe smiled. He offered Isla his arm. "I believe now is the time when we should greet our guests."

"Your guests," she said. "You arranged it."

"With some help," he said. He touched his pocket, conscious of the ring inside. He was eager to propose to Flora, but he would wait until after the ball. Isla deserved that. He didn't want anyone to speaking about anything except how beautiful his sister was.

"You look magnificent," he said.

"It's really no effort," she said nonchalantly, but her eyes sparkled, and he knew he'd made her happy.

She wore a ruby colored dress that glimmered in the light. Black lace was embroidered around the neckline which was rather lower than he thought appropriate, though he wasn't going to begin the ball by questioning her on that. There were some things one shouldn't discuss.

"That color is very festive," he said.

"Oh?" She waved a fan.

"It's almost as if you truly like Christmas," he said.

"Perhaps this was a good idea. It was quite amusing to look for this." She glanced at the ceiling and at the many garlands. "I do wonder what our parents would make of all this."

"Most likely they would lecture about how this is a fire hazard."

"Yes. They were always sensible."

"Perhaps," he said. "But they weren't always kind."

Isla squeezed his hand. "You've made things up to Callum," she said gently.

"Do you mind that I gave him back the castle Father took from him? I should perhaps have asked you, but—"

She shook her head. "No. It was good you did that."

More people streamed into the room. The musicians played a minuet, and some enthusiastic party-goers began to dance.

"This is quite the grandest ball the Highlands has ever seen, my dear brother," Isla said.

He grinned proudly. "Ah, yes. I am glad you think that."

"What some of these people want all the way in the Highlands is beyond me. I'm sure they don't all have relatives here."

"Perhaps some of them desire to spend time with you," Wolfe said gently.

"Oh. I see. Is that why there are so many eligible men here?"

"I'm glad you found them eligible too."

FLORA CONTINUED TO move about the room, making certain everything was lovely. People laughed and danced. Some exclaimed over the Christmas tree, and others marveled at the yule log.

Her heart still raced, pondering Wolfe's strange desire to dance with her. He'd abandoned her easily once his sister and friends arrived. Why would he want to dance a waltz? They'd danced a waltz together before, and it had been intimate and incredible, and not something she could dance before hundreds of guests without revealing just how much she cared for him.

Wolfe's gaze seemed to be often on her. He was standing before the Christmas tree now, speaking with one of the musicians. He turned toward her, and she abruptly averted her gaze, but not before she saw a smile spread on his lips.

How on earth was she going to forget his smile? She hadn't forgotten him ever since she was a child, and she knew him so much better now.

"Ladies and gentlemen," Wolfe announced, and the room quieted. "I would like to announce, that we have a talented artist with us tonight."

Some people clapped.

"The most talented artist in fact, that I have ever met."

Murmurings sounded, and he beamed.

Her heart fluttered. This wasn't in the schedule.

"I've been to many concerts over the years," he said. "But it is my supreme honor to introduce Miss Flora Schmidt."

He intended her to...play?

He strode toward her. "Come, Flora."

"Are you certain, my lord?"

"I couldn't be more certain." He led her to the piano, and leaned toward her. "The others will accompany you."

"The other..."

"Musicians." He smiled. "I want you to have your moment. Those compositions are not just for the piano. I want you to hear what your music sounds like. Whatever else happens, I want you to have this moment."

"What else do you exactly intend to happen?"

His eyes glimmered. "One surprise at a time, sweetheart."

She sat down at the piano.

"You mustn't look so surprised to be here," Wolfe said. "You're the very best pianist I know."

Right. Of course. He admired her talent. That was all. He would admire her talent even if she were a hoary-haired octogenarian man, and he would likely gush about the same enthusiasm about his discovery. If she weren't here, he would laud his performers instead.

Naturally he would laud her performance. He lauded everything.

Her heart ached. Something about his boyish enthusiasm was appealing, and she could see how he'd managed to create a gaming hell, even when he'd been young, even when so many people must have been shocked, and even when many people must have doubted his vision. No one had thought many people would come all the way to the Highlands for a Christmas ball, but evidently they had.

He'd radiated charisma, and she'd fallen for it, even though the one thing servant girls whispered to one another was that one should never ever be taken advantage of by the master. One should never listen to their praise, one should never think it was something more.

She'd considered herself intelligent, and she'd laughed at being told something so obvious.

But here she was. She'd fallen for it.

At least Wolfe and she had taken precautions, but she didn't know if that made her feel better, because even though it was mad, she still thought about him, still yearned to lie in his arms again.

"I would speak more, but you have an audience."

She nodded and her heart thundered.

The room was quiet, and Flora placed her fingers on the piano keys. Her heart beat madly, and she wondered how she might ever remember to play the notes at the correct tempo if even the simple influx and outflux of breath seemed challenging. The glossy white and black keys remained enticing, remained familiar, even if the large ballroom filled with onlookers was not.

And so she played.

She played notes she'd scribbled while working at the vicarage and in London, she played notes from her heart, and then, most incredibly, the musicians joined her.

Wolfe must have found her music and hand copied it for them. He hadn't only been entertaining guests. He'd been thinking of her.

He was right. Soon she would go to Cornwall, but now she could enjoy playing her music with so many others. She wasn't in London. She was safe.

CHAPTER TWENTY-ONE

FLORA FINISHED PLAYING. She rose from the piano. The music was finished, but it had been replaced by a new sound, that of applause.

It thundered through the room.

Her heart sang, and she moved from the piano, into the thick crowd of people.

A hand grabbed onto her.

Wolfe.

Of course he was there beside her, and her heart warmed.

In the next moment she was pushed behind the Christmas tree, and then behind the balcony.

"Hello... Miss Schmidt." The voice didn't belong to Wolfe or any of the footmen and male servants, and a shiver shot through her spine.

It's him.

She didn't want to look at him. She didn't want to confirm what every nerve ending seemed to naturally know: that it was him, the man who killed her father and who could only want to harm her.

Where was Wolfe? She needed to find him. He always made her feel safe.

"Don't leave," Mr. Warne said. Something glinted in the moonlight.

A knife.

She inhaled sharply.

"If you try to leave, I'll be compelled to hurt you. You don't want that, do you?"

She shook her head rapidly, staring at the knife.

"How odd," Mr. Warne remarked. "Back in London you went by a different name. I suppose you were ashamed of your father."

She swung her head at him. "Leave my father out of this."

He grinned. "Ah. It is really you. I am certain. I thought it doubtful two women could play the piano so beautifully."

"Many people play the piano beautifully," she said.

"You are too humble. Besides, those were your own compositions, were they not? You always did consider yourself a composer. Foolish child and now foolish woman."

She stiffened.

"Come with me now," he said, his voice suave and gentle.

"I couldn't possibly," she said.

"You think anyone notices you?" the man continued, clasping onto her hand. "Do you think you're special?"

"No."

"You're a servant. No one notices a missing servant." The man forced her toward the balcony. In the next moment he opened the door and shoved her outside into the cool air.

Perhaps she could escape. Perhaps she could scream. Perhaps—

Something cold that she recognized as a barrel pressed into her back.

"Now, don't do anything crazy," he said. "Better you just die than to suffer more."

"Is it?" she asked, "if it means they catch you?"

His eyes twinkled. "You don't want to know what I can do. Might go after that earl of yours. You were making eyes at him quite a bit. As if a man like him would notice a woman like you."

"You followed me here and you somehow weaseled your way into an invitation," Flora said.

"Nonsense," Mr. Warne said. "I didn't need to do that."

"You have some magical powers? These are good people. You shouldn't be here."

"I thought you knew more than that," Mr. Warne said. "I was invited here. Finding you was a fortunate coincidence."

Flora blinked.

"You didn't know? These are my friends."

Her eyes widened farther.

"I often go with the host to concerts together," Mr. Warne said.

"You did always like music."

"Like it? I was good at it."

"Then why did you murder your piano tutor?" Flora asked.

"That had nothing to do with music. Now, I'm thinking, I could just kill you right here and be done with you."

"What if someone finds the body?" she asked smugly.

"I'll hide it."

"You think people won't notice? There are couples skating on the lake below," Flora said.

There weren't, but he didn't need to know that.

"Is that so?"

She raised her chin. "There are all sorts of festive activities. It's Christmas after all."

"Well, luckily, I'm not planning on taking you on a walk around the estate. I imagine you already know it too well. We're going to enter my carriage and drive from here. And if you say anything, I won't hesitate to kill the groom outside. He looks pretty young. Thirteen? Fourteen?"

Flora's heart sank.

The man had murdered before.

SOON IT WOULD BE THE waltz. Wolfe went in search of Flora, but he did not see her. He frowned and asked some of the footmen. They hadn't seen her since her piano performance.

She was gone.

The ballroom was filled with people, but none of them were her. No one had her precise facial shape, and no one had her precise form.

Why would she leave now? Was it possible she didn't want to dance with him, didn't want to be with him?

He despised the hint of doubt that drifted through him, twisting his organs in odd manners, so that he felt simultaneously nauseous and faint.

Wolfe clenched his fists. He had no intention of spending the rest of his life knowing he'd met the perfect person for himself, one who shared his interests, and that he'd let her walk from his very own ballroom.

"Isla," he said, drawing his sister from a bevy of men.

"Brother dear?"

"Come talk with me," he said abruptly and pulled her away.

"You know, I thought the whole point of this affair was to get me to talk with these men, who are quite interesting in fact. Do you know anything about Lord Terrence?"

"I don't have time to discuss that," Wolfe said. "Where is Flora?"

"Your Christmas consultant? Your bedtime companion?" Isla frowned. "I don't know. Is it so important?"

Wolfe sucked in a deep breath of air, though the fact didn't manage to calm his thundering heart. Perhaps she really had run away.

"You needn't look so upset," Isla said. "This is a fine evening. I was wrong to say otherwise. I'm actually enjoying this evening, and I do like the Christmas theme even though I did think it was quite silly before."

"You did?" Wolfe blinked. "You mean I didn't even need a Christmas theme?" He shook his head. "Anyway. That's not the point. Flora is missing."

"She's probably just doing something behind the scenes," Isla said.

"No, she's been gone too long, and we were going to waltz together."

Isla's eyes widened. "You were going to waltz with the maid? I know you bedded her, but—"

"I love her," Wolfe said. "I adore her. And after the ball, I was going to propose to her."

"Oh." Isla blinked.

"The waltz has already happened though."

"Perhaps that's for the best." Isla averted her eyes, and her hands fluttered uncharacteristically. "After all, she's not of our class. She's not educated."

"Her father was a court musician for years. He wasn't exactly penniless, and she knows the *ton's* desires as well as any society woman."

"Yes, I do see that," Isla said. "She arranges events with the aplomb one rather expects of a countess."

"I'm glad you see that too," Wolfe said. "Though I'm not marrying her for her prowess in etiquette."

"Why don't you speak with the grooms outside?" Isla suggested.

"She wouldn't have left. She doesn't have a form of transport."

"Perhaps she was not alone."

CHAPTER TWENTY-TWO

THE COACH MOVED OVER the snow. Now would be a wonderful time for a snowstorm.

Actually, a snowstorm wouldn't do. Flora wanted a blizzard.

The kind rumored to occur in Upper Canada and the more removed sections of the foreign colonies. The kind where they measured the snowfall in feet rather than inches. The kind where one could only go outside if one had a rope firmly attached to one's waist, and even then, one couldn't wander for long lest one find one's toes frozen.

Unfortunately the weather had been pleasant all day.

"They'll find you," Flora said. "You can't get away with this."

Mr. Warne smiled. "I don't know what kind of idealistic notions you have. But they have no basis in reality. You're like your father. He thought he was too important too. But he wasn't."

She stiffened. "Why did you kill him?"

He grinned. "I knew you saw me. Good thing I went after you."

"It was brutal."

He shrugged. "I wouldn't worry about that. Any death with a knife involves a bit of blood. No more brutal than other ways to die, I can assure you. I might use one of the more creative manners for you." There was a strange tone in his voice she detested immediately.

"Your father was spying on me," Mr. Warne continued. "He was using me, even though *I* was *his* employer. I never thought that I'd have to kill him and I'm sorry that you had to see it. I think we both know why you have to die."

"They'll find out."

Mr. Warne laughed. "Once again, these are my friends."

"They'll find out I was missing. They'll worry about me."

He shook his head. "Are you certain? They might have wanted you to play as some entertainment, some novelty, a girl pianist *not* part of the *ton*, but I assure you that is the end of their interest. I might even tell them that you were upset and fled early. Perhaps you were embarrassed by the poor music."

"It wasn't poor," she said. "It was wonderful."

"Oh? I'm not going to compliment you, dearie."

She knew.

She didn't care what he thought, but his words still stung. Would people believe it if he did say that? Was this the end?

"What did you do with my father?"

"Oh, you don't know? He fancied himself as caring about the war. He was passing information about us to the British. Can you imagine that? We were just trying to make a living. We weren't harming people. Creating jobs isn't that bad."

"You were a smuggler," Flora said softly, realizing it for the first time.

"Quite. Your father was going to report me."

"But smuggling is bad. It prolonged the war," Flora said.

"He wanted to destroy *my* life."

"He wouldn't have killed you."

"You underestimate the importance of a good reputation," Mr. Warne said.

WOLFE WOULD JUST LOOK for her outside. That was it. He rushed through the ballroom and told his surprised-looking butler to get his coat and boots. He then poked his head outdoors and waved until the grooms, who were managing the coaches, appeared.

"Have you seen Miss Flora Schmidt?"

They nodded.

"She left."

"Alone?" His heart squeezed.

The grooms looked at each other, and shifted their legs. *Devil it.* Perhaps they'd heard rumors about Flora and himself.

"It's very important you tell the truth," Wolfe said. "No one will get in trouble. *Flora* won't get in trouble. In fact, she may be in danger."

Wolfe wished he didn't believe the latter. She couldn't be in danger, he told himself. Perhaps someone desired to harm her, but that person was in London, hundreds of miles away.

"She was with a man," one of the grooms said finally.

"Who was it?"

They looked at each other.

Finally, one said, "Mr. Warne."

Mr. Warne.

A man he'd invited all the way from London. A man who loved music. A man who had been asking questions about Flora at the public house.

Guilt gnawed him. He shouldn't have surprised Flora. He'd put her in unspeakable danger. Was she already dead? Did he want to kill her in a location that would not involve staining his conveyance?

"Can you describe the coach?"

"Well, it's a black coach, my lord. Shiny."

"No family crest?"

They shook their heads.

"Devil it," he said.

Well.

It would be fine. He would go after them. The horse wouldn't like the snow, but perhaps he could catch up.

"How long ago did they leave?"

"Reckon it's been ten minutes."

Devil it.

No matter. He could catch up with them. He had to.

The butler came quickly, thank goodness, and he put on his coat and boots. The butler had also had the foresight to include a hat and gloves.

"Would you like me to inform anyone at the ball of your absence, my lord?"

"I—"

"It is possible that they might find your absence distressing."

Right. He was the host after all.

What was he going to do? Was he going to find it by himself? What if he chose the wrong road at some point?

This was supposed to be the most wonderful ball in the world. How could he disrupt it? But Flora was more important.

Instead he rushed to the ball. Everyone needed to help. It would be too easy to lose her otherwise. He rushed into the room, spotting the footmen carrying delightful dishes. He grabbed a drink from the footman and a spoon and clanged them together.

"Excuse me! Excuse me! May I have your attention?" he said.

The room gradually stilled.

"It's a very fine ball you're having here, my lord," one of the men from the public house said.

"Aye," said another. "Speech! Speech!"

They thought he wanted to bask in the glory of the ball. But he had something more important to tell them.

"I am sorry to inform you that Miss Schmidt, the woman who played the piano for you and who composed the most magnificent music, has been abducted."

A few men blinked.

"We ain't in the war any longer," one of the rougher men said. "No one should be capturing anyone."

"That may be so," Wolfe said. "And it is true that capturings are rare occurrences, but I'm afraid Miss Schmidt has been taken by Mr. Warne."

The crowd murmured. His sister and friends appeared shocked.

"I need your help," Wolfe said. "They left fifteen minutes ago. I don't know which direction they took, but if we split up, perhaps we can find them. We must find them."

"That lovely girl has been taken?" one of the men from the public house said. "That's horrible, my lord."

"We'll help you, my lord," another man hollered.

"Obviously it's not mandatory," Wolfe said, "but I would be ever so grateful."

And then the room filled with noise and everyone rushed forward.

Isla strode toward him. "She's really been taken?"

He nodded to her solemnly.

"Perhaps it's some sort of misunderstanding," Lord Pierce said, who Wolfe noticed had been staying very close to Isla all evening.

"No." Wolfe shook his head. "It's something else."

"Perhaps they desire to be alone," Lord Pierce said gently, not quite meeting Wolfe's eyes.

"No," Wolfe said flatly. "They have a past, and there's a reason why he would want to harm her."

"In that case, let's go."

FLORA'S HEART SEEMED to be permanently lodged in her throat.

She was opposite Mr. Warne, the man who'd changed her life so completely.

Was he going to decide now that they were far enough from the manor house that he could kill her? Did he want to do it in a quiet location away from his driver? Or was his driver someone who would be happy to assist? Perhaps he was one of those former smugglers from Sussex.

Would keeping him talking be a good idea? Did he enjoy having a listener to whom he could tell his deeds without fear of reprisal, confident that he would soon murder her? Or would it hasten his desire?

THE EARL'S CHRISTMAS CONSULTANT 169

The driver slowed, and irritation spread on Mr. Warne's face. He hammered on the roof. "What's going on? I said hurry!"

Voices sounded from outside.

Flora doubted that the driver had developed a sudden proclivity to speak to himself.

"Hurry up!" Mr. Warne shouted again. "Go! Go!"

The door opened, and Wolfe stood before her. "Now, Mr. Warne, so eager to leave? I thought you said you enjoyed Scotland."

"Good evening, my lord," Mr. Warne said hastily. "I—er—"

"Don't have a response?" Wolfe finished for him. "Perhaps you can think of one when you are driven to the magistrate."

"I don't need to go to the magistrate," Mr. Warne said. "What nonsense. What *utter* nonsense."

"I think you do," Wolfe said sternly. "For killing this lady's father and for attempting to kill her."

"You can't prove it," Mr. Warne said. "I just wanted to have a romantic evening with this *servant*."

"I would suggest," Flora said, "that you also inform the magistrate that Mr. Warne was involved in a large smuggling operation. I think they might find that very interesting."

"Nonsense," Mr. Warne sputtered, but his voice seemed to grow more nervous.

"Did you hear that?" Wolfe turned and spoke to some people behind him. "This man also smuggled."

He extended his hand to Flora. "Come sweetheart."

WOLFE PULLED FLORA from the carriage and into his arms.

He'd found her, with the help of the guests at his ball. They'd taken shortcuts to put up barricades on all these roads, and luckily they'd caught Mr. Warne.

"I love you, Flora," he said. He said the words again. "I love you," testing them out.

She stared at him, uncertain, as if she couldn't quite believe what he'd said. He said it again, just in case something had happened to her hearing. "I love you," he said a third time.

Her eyes became dewy, and he realized tears had formed over her eyes.

"I should have told you before," he said. "This isn't the first time I've thought it."

"You don't mean it."

"I do. I think I've loved you ever since that first day when you came here."

"Not when you discovered me learning French grammar."

Wolfe blushed. "It may have been more romantic if I'd said that."

Flora laughed. "It was French grammar. It hardly gives one the feeling of romance." She tilted her head. "How did you know where I was?"

"I didn't. I was searching for you. We all were."

"But this is your ball. I know how much it costs to put on, and I know how badly you want it to be a success. To have all the guests tramping around in the snow..."

"They had a memorable ball," he said. "But for me, it's the most wonderful ball of my life."

"Is that so?"

He nodded. "The first part wasn't the best part," he said. "But I have high hopes for the next part."

"Indeed?" her voice trembled.

In the next moment he knelt down into the snow. It was cold, and it was wet, but he couldn't care less. All that mattered was Flora. "Flora, will you do me the honor of becoming my wife? You're already in my heart and I want you to be by my side forever and ever and ever."

"Wolfe," she murmured.

"Will you marry me, Flora?"

"Yes," she breathed, and he beamed.

"Well then, I think we should return to the manor house." He swept her into his arms and carried her to his carriage.

"My dress is dirty."

"I'll buy you a new dress."

"I'm getting your clothes dirty."

"Don't worry." He took her into his carriage, and they arrived back at the manor house. He carried her in his arms and headed for the ballroom.

"You're not taking me upstairs?"

"You want to? I think that sounds quite good." His voice sounded husky.

"I hadn't meant that," she said, and butterflies danced in her chest now. "What did you mean?"

"We still need to have a dance at the ball," he said.

"But..."

"The musicians are still there, I believe. The guests will come."

They walked into the ballroom. The room was filled with people, and they cheered when they saw her.

"You found her!"

"I certainly did," Wolfe said. "May I present the future Countess of McIntyre to you."

The room cheered, though he noted the confusion on Hamish and Callum's faces. They always had been a bit blind, even if they were good at math.

He put her on the floor.

"We're dancing for everyone now."

The musicians played a joyful dance because they were united and everyone danced together, hopping and turning. It was a country dance, requiring frequent changes of partners. Everyone was happy at her presence. No one dismissed her, and she realized she'd gained so much more than just a husband. She'd gained a community and she'd gained a home.

Then the musicians played a Christmas song, and for a moment the dancers were unsure how to approach it. Then the earl, her betrothed, began to twirl her in his arms, just as if they were dancing a waltz, and other couples followed them. It was Christmas, and magic had happened.

The ballroom was rather more untidy than it had been before. Some people were in muddy boots, and some had not changed from slippers to boots when they went outside. Their clothes were disheveled, and others had simply tossed their cloaks on the floor. It was messy and unlike anything a ball should be, and yet it was entirely perfect all the same.

CHAPTER TWENTY-THREE

FLORA WAS SAFE AND at his side. Wolfe squeezed her hand.

Last night had been a smattering of conventions. Nothing had mattered except ensuring her safety and proclaiming his love to her.

His heart swelled. It had seemed to have expanded these past weeks, as if he'd realized not only how wonderful Flora was, but also how wonderful everything else was.

Right now it was wonderful to be in his room. It was wonderful to hear the chirps of the countryside, and not the bustle of curricles bounding down his street on the way to Hyde Park and the angry cries of other drivers.

The Duke and Duchess of Vernon and Lord and Lady Hamish Montgomery had all elected to spend the night at McIntyre Manor after the ball, and they were occupying the various guest rooms. And yet, Wolfe vowed never to spend another night without Flora. The nights before the ball, after Isla had arrived, had been dreadful.

Flora had slept soundly beside him throughout the night, clinging to him, but now she stirred.

"Sweetheart." He kissed her head, and then watched as her eyes opened. Her lips swerved into a slow smile that tugged his heart, and he made a decision to devote the next few minutes to kissing her.

Footsteps sounded on the corridor, and Flora pulled herself from his arms. "I suppose we should dress."

"Right."

Wolfe followed Flora's gaze to the elaborate gown, now stained with mud and damp from snow.

A knock sounded on the door, and Wolfe stiffened. He then grabbed his robe and went to answer the door, opening it only a crack.

His sister stood before him

"Isla..." He broke off. Was she going to berate him? The ball had been intended to highlight the strengths of the McIntyre family, but it was possible that she might take a less romantic view of last night's search party. Having one's older brother publicly declare his affections for a servant and usher everyone outside for an impromptu search party when they were wearing their finest attire was perhaps not the best way to impress the *ton*.

He swallowed hard. "I'm sorry."

She raised her impeccably plucked eyebrows, and he braced himself for a tirade. Instead she said, "Whatever for?"

"I don't think you selected a husband."

"Well, that was perhaps your fault for inviting a brutal murderer to court me."

His face must have fallen, for her eyes softened.

"It was a lovely ball, Wolfe, and it was sweet of you to hold it."

"That's what you came to tell me?"

"Well, I'm not nearly that polite," she said. "I'd intended to mention it to you over breakfast. I came to give you this." She handed him a dark, folded piece of fabric, and he stared at it."

"It's a dress, Wolfe. I assume Flora doesn't want to wear last night's dirtied gown."

He blinked. "So you don't mind?"

"Of course, I don't," she said. "I've only ever wanted you to be happy."

"You know, I think I had it more correct when I was younger," Wolfe mused. "My instinct then was that you should never marry, because no one will be good enough for you."

"You really believe that?"

"Of course I do."

"Then why have you been pressing me to marry?"

"I didn't want your reputation to be ruined because of what happened with Callum. You don't need to marry," he said. "We're not exactly poor."

"Hmm... I thought I could be more involved in Hades' Lair."

"That's a gaming hell," he said. "You can't be involved in that."

"But it is most interesting. The decorating, the accounting..."

"Oh, you would say the decorating is interesting. Perhaps you could be some sort of liaison, but you're not allowed to be at the tables. And you know, that does not help your reputation."

"I do not want to marry a man who wants me to remain at home. There must be some advantages to having money."

"Yes." He smiled. "But I did think you desired to marry after the spectacle with dear Callum ended so poorly."

"It's in the past now."

"IS THERE A CELEBRATION in here?" The duke's voice sailed through the open door, and Flora scrambled up.

She wasn't supposed to be here. She was in bed, with an earl.

But then she remembered that Wolfe had proposed, and that most everything in the world was good again.

Her father was no longer alive, but at least his murder would be avenged. His discovery on Mr. Warne's unsavory method of building his wealth would ensure that Mr. Warne would no longer trouble her.

"I feel I must apologize to you," Lady Isla said. "We were good friends once, and I want us to be friends again."

Flora nodded, too astonished to say anything else.

"I would like to welcome you to our family," Isla continued.

"That means so much," Flora murmured.

"Oh, you needn't look so shocked," Isla said. "I am your sister after all."

Flora beamed.

"I want everyone out of the room," Wolfe declared. "We'll join you in the breakfast room."

Isla and the duke left the room, and Wolfe swept her into a long, deep and utterly delightful, kiss.

"I'm looking forward to the first of many, many mornings with you," he said.

THE EARL'S CHRISTMAS CONSULTANT 177

"What do you say to having a honeymoon in Paris?" Wolfe asked. "You can use your French skills."

Flora did her best to scowl at him.

"Italy," Wolfe said quickly. "I meant Italy. We can visit the Duke and Duchess of Alfriston. I think you'll like the duchess. She has distinct bluestocking tendencies that you'll approve of."

"We can go to France," she said. "Just don't tell the inhabitants that—"

"—you were pretending to be French for four years?"

Flora flushed. "Yes. That would be something not to tell them."

Wolfe laughed. "Very well, sweetheart. I'm so glad that you were my Christmas consultant."

They had met twice before, but if it hadn't been for Christmas, they wouldn't be engaged now. Happiness soared through Flora.

EPILOGUE

A TRUMPET WAS PLAYING the most wonderful music in the world. Well, it was *almost* the most wonderful music in the world.

No music equaled Wolfe's bride's music, but the musician *was* playing the Trumpet Voluntary as Flora marched down the aisle of St. George's Church, and Wolfe would allow him many extra points.

Wolfe's heart thrummed merrily, as his wife-to-be approached him. Curled locks lined the sides of her face. They swayed as she marched toward him.

Wolfe had elected to marry Flora in London. He wanted everyone to see just how lovely she was. He wasn't going to allow her to be some item of gossip, the lady's maid who'd become a countess. He'd wanted to give her a wedding befitting that of a countess.

"I love you," he said, as she stepped toward him, and he offered her his hand.

The priest cleared his throat, as if reminding him that that particular line wasn't scripted, but Wolfe could hardly care whether it was in the ceremony or not.

"I love you," he repeated again, as Flora clasped his hand. "I love you."

"Well," the priest said, and then entered into his speech.

The ceremony was short, and yet every word seemed precious. There was no one in the world he would rather tie himself with than Flora.

"You may kiss the bride," the priest said.

Wolfe smiled. At one time the words would have horrified people. His bride might be somewhat unconventional. When he gazed into the rows of Wolfe's family and friends, he saw only happiness in their gazes.

He pulled Flora toward him. His life wasn't supposed to be in some elaborately decorated gaming hell with men who paid to be there. Soon his place would be in Scotland, playing piano with his wife in the evening.

ABOUT THE AUTHOR

BORN IN TEXAS, BIANCA Blythe spent four years in England. She worked in a fifteenth century castle, though sadly that didn't actually involve spotting dukes and earls strutting about in Hessians.

She credits British weather for forcing her into a library, where she discovered her first Julia Quinn novel. Thank goodness for blustery downpours.

Bianca now lives in California with her husband.

WEDDING TROUBLE
- Don't Tie the Knot
- Dukes Prefer Bluestockings
- The Earl's Christmas Consultant
- How to Train a Viscount
- A Kiss for the Marquess
- A Holiday Proposal

MATCHMAKING FOR WALLFLOWERS
- How to Capture a Duke
- A Rogue to Avoid

Runaway Wallflower
Mad About the Baron
A Marquess for Convenience
The Wrong Heiress for Christmas

THE SLEUTHING STARLET
Murder at the Manor House
Danger on the Downs
The Body in Bloomsbury
A Continental Murder

Made in United States
Orlando, FL
12 June 2023